William Black

Adventures in Thule

William Black

Adventures in Thule

ISBN/EAN: 9783337339951

Printed in Europe, USA, Canada, Australia, Japan

Cover: Foto ©Andreas Hilbeck / pixelio.de

More available books at **www.hansebooks.com**

ADVENTURES IN THULE

THREE STORIES FOR BOYS

WILLIAM BLACK

NEW AND REVISED EDITION

LONDON

SAMPSON LOW, MARSTON & COMPANY
LIMITED

St. Dunstan's House

1894

CONTENTS.

.

AN ADVENTURE IN THULE.

B

AN ADVENTURE IN THULE.

CHAPTER I.

HIGH up on one of the headlands of the Island of Lewis two young lads were idly seated on the grass, sometimes plucking a head of Dutch clover, sometimes turning their eyes to a group of small islands which lay far out at the horizon line, beyond the wide blue spaces of the Atlantic. It was a warm, still, beautiful day. The sea was calm; those low-lying islands out there were faint and pale like clouds.

" Archie," said the elder (speaking in Gaelic, of which the following is a translation), " I saw one of the French smacks go by this morning."

" I saw her too," replied the younger lad, who was the schoolmaster's son.

There was nothing said for a time. The bees hummed amongst the clover; the collie lying near sleepily winked his eyes; and Colin

M'Calmont, the taller of the two lads, kept his gaze directed on the pale blue islands out at the horizon.   At length he said,—

"Archie, my father is a hard-working man; and it is not easy now to make the farms pay, with the rents high and sheep not selling well at the market.   My father has not his troubles to seek, as the minister says.   And to think that these Frenchmen should be allowed to go and kill a sheep, just as they want it, when they are going by Farriskeir or Rua; that is what angers me."

"And me too," said Archie Livingston, "though it is not my father's sheep they kill. It angers me because they are Frenchmen; yes, and thieves beside.   But what can you do, Colin ? "

They were still regarding the far islands.

"If my father would let me," M'Calmont said, "I'd go out and live on Farriskeir until all the French smacks had gone by to Iceland.   If they knew any one was on Farriskeir or Rua, that would be enough.   They would soon talk about it amongst themselves, and there would be no more stealing of my father's sheep.   Do you think I would be afraid ?   I would not be afraid.

I would build myself a hut, for there is plenty of wood washed up since the big vessel went ashore on Rua."

"Colin," said the other, after a while, "I have something to tell you. Do you know my horse-pistol?"

"Of course I know it."

"Would it not be a fine thing, now, if you and I were to go out to Farriskeir and hide behind the rocks, and when the Frenchmen were coming near we might have a shot at them?"

"Yes, and maybe kill some one," said the other, scornfully. "That would be a fine thing. It would be a fine thing to be hanged."

"How could they hang you for that?" said the schoolmaster's son. "If a man comes into your house to steal your money, you may shoot at him; and if he comes to your island to steal your sheep, why not the same? Besides, he is a Frenchman. The sheriff at Stornoway would not say anything to you for shooting at a Frenchman."

"I don't know that. I am not going to try," said the elder lad, with a grim sort of smile. "But I will tell you now, Archie, what would be a fine thing. Do you think we could slip away to Farriskeir without being seen? There is no one going down to the boat just now; they would not miss it at all. And if any one were asking for us, would they not think we had gone up to the shieling with bread for Mary and Ailasa and the rest of them? Well, now, if we could slip away out to Farriskeir and lie behind the rocks, just as you were saying, and if one of the French boats was to come near, where would be the harm in giving a shot in the air? Do you see that now? For they would not dare to land; and when they got up to Reikjavik in Iceland they would tell all the other boats that they had been fired at, and that people lived on Farriskeir and Rua-veg now; and not another Frenchman would ever come near the place again. Do you see that now? They would go away up to Reikjavik, and they would say, 'There is to be no more stealing a sheep from Farriskeir and making a laugh over it. They have people on Farriskeir now.' And the Frenchmen can understand each other very well, though no one else can make out what they say."

"I will go with you, Colin; we will try it!"

said the other, eagerly. "My father will not be back from Stornoway till the Friday night. But about the powder, Colin; I have no powder, and you cannot fire the horse-pistol without powder."

However, there were a great many things to be thought of besides getting powder before this exploit could be ventured upon; and they set about completing these details according to their different temperaments; the younger lad, who was a great reader of books, filled with an eager delight at the romance of the enterprise; the elder animated chiefly by a sober determination that he would do what he could to prevent any more of his father's sheep being stolen. Indeed, it was not until late in the afternoon that Colin M'Calmont found time to make his way up Glen-Estera, to Sir Evan Roy's shooting-box there, that he might beg some gunpowder of Dugald M'Lean, the gamekeeper.

He found M'Lean—who was the sole occupant of the lodge at this time of the year—seated on the bank of the stream that flowed past the house. He was contentedly smoking his pipe and regarding a noble salmon that lay on the grass, while his rod was not far off. Colin had

to pull his wits together in addressing the
keeper, who had not the best of tempers.

"Eh, but that's a fine fish, Mr. M'Lean!"
said he—the rest of the people called the keeper
plain Dugald, so this was a cunning compliment.
"That is a fine fish indeed. I have heard them
saying there was not a better salmon-fisher in
the Lews than yourself. They were saying you
could throw a fly eight-and-thirty yards. Some
day I will be asking you to teach me how to
throw a fly."

"You will be better minding your own
business at the farm," said the keeper, rather
gruffly (and also speaking in Gaelic). "What
brings you to Glen-Estera?"

"There is not much doing at the farm at this
time of the year. I was thinking, Mr. M'Lean,
that perhaps you could spare me a little gunpowder."

"Gunpowder!" the keeper exclaimed, angrily.
"To make *pioyes** of and set your father's barn
on fire? It is a fool that you are, Colin, and

* The word *pioyes* is applied in Scotland to a small cone
made of gunpowder kneaded with water until the powder
forms a sort of paste. When the tip of the cone is lit it
begins to splutter and hiss like a miniature Vesuvius.

more, to think that I will be giving you any
gunpowder ! "

"Indeed, it's you who are wrong, then, Mr.
M'Lean, to think that I was wanting gunpowder
for *pioyes*," said Colin, sturdily. "I am no
longer at school; it is not *pioyes* that I am
thinking of." And then he cast about for an
excuse. "I am sure there is no one who knows
better than yourself of the mischief that the
hoodies* make."

"Oh," continued the boy, "they are the mischievous birds! The young grouse—the young
black game—have no peace for them; but worse
than that is the time of the eggs in the spring-
time. Surely you will know, Mr. M'Lean, that
when a young lad is looking after the sheep he
has many chances of seeing the nests."

And here it seemed suddenly to strike the
keeper that he was neglecting one of the chief
elements of his business—which was to keep on
friendly terms with the men and lads about the
different farms.

"Now that is a good thing I am told about
you, Colin, my lad," said he, in quite a different

---

* Hoodies are a species of crow held in much disfavour
by the preservers of game in the Highlands.

tone; "that you do not take the eggs for
foolishness or mischief, and that you do not let
the dogs chase the young coveys or the hares;
and that you are a sensible lad, and you may
have a farm yourself some day from Sir Evan."

"It is not wrong what you have heard about
the nests," said Colin, modestly. "And I keep
in the dogs, too, though the young dogs are
eager after the hares. And I was saying about
the hoodies; Archie Livingston has a pistol, and
if you were to be giving me a little gunpowder
from time to time, I think I could kill a hoodie
or two when there was nothing doing but the
minding of the sheep."

The keeper rose to his feet.

"There is a job for you, Colin, my lad. Bring
the fish into the house, and I will give you some
powder."

Very joyously did Colin obey; for besides his
immediate want being supplied, he had now
before him the prospect of unlimited stalking
expeditions—along the shore and up over the
rocks after the detested hoodie-crows. And if
he did not tell Dugald M'Lean for what immediate purpose he wanted some powder, it was
because he knew very well that M'Lean would

instantly speak of the matter and compel him to abandon so dangerous an enterprise.

They went into the lodge, and the keeper, who was now quite friendly in his gruff way, gave him some powder in a small tin canister, and even offered him some percussion caps too; but M'Calmont explained that the horse-pistol was fired by flint and steel. Then he set out on his way down Glen-Estera again.

When he got back to the coast and near to the headland which has been mentioned, instead of ascending the height, he went down and struck across some broad white sands which in former times were no doubt covered by the sea. Then he reached a belt of rock facing the Atlantic, and in a small sheltered creek discovered Archie Livingston busy at work overhauling the small sailing-boat that lay at its moorings there. Archie looked up startled, for he had not heard his friend's approach— the sands being soft to the foot.

"They are often saying that Dugald M'Lean is an uncivil man," Colin M'Calmont remarked, as he stepped into the boat that his companion had now shoved alongside the rock, " but he is not that. He has given me a good deal of

powder, and I am to have more, too, for shooting
the hoodies ; and I think you and I, Archie, will
have many a good day after the hoodies.   They
do not fly so quick as the birds the gentlemen
go after ; but they are a great deal more
cunning, and it is not easy to get at them.   He
is not an uncivil man at all, but a very civil
man ; and he knows that we do not let the dogs
chase the young birds.   Did you bring down the
bottle of water, Archie ? "

" Oh yes, I brought down the bottle of water,
and it's in the locker.   And I have gone all over
the boat, Colin, and tried the sheets ; and if I
were you, it is a new topping-lift I would be
having."

But Colin did not seem quite reassured by the
fact that his younger companion had inspected
the vessel that was to carry them away from the
land in the morning ; so now, in the gathering
dusk, he set to work himself and had a thorough
investigation.

" The topping-lift will do very well," said he,
" for it is not in any gale that we are going.
With a north wind or a south wind I will go ;
with an east wind or a west wind I will not go.
If we were to be beating against a wind either

going or coming, would not some one see us, sooner or later? And you know very well, Archie, that it is not a sure thing that we may see any French smack come near, though now is the time of their passing; and that would be a fine thing to have all the people making a joke of us, and saying,—' Look at the boys that went out to frighten the Frenchmen and came running back without seeing any.' I would not like that, neither would you; but it is I that would have to do the quarrelling, if there was any quarrelling. But now, if there is a nice steady wind from either north or south in the morning, then we will run away out in a short time and get the boat hidden in a creek at Farriskeir; and the topping-lift will do very well;" and with that he gave another haul at it, swinging the end of the boom up into the air.

Now when everything had been made fast and secure for their voyage on the morrow—the mainsail having been lowered and stowed— Archie was called upon to produce the weapon which was to give a wholesome warning to the French fishermen to avoid for the future the shores of Farriskeir and its adjacent islands. It

was a large cavalry pistol, somewhat dilapidated,
but showing traces of ancient adornment.
Archie had freshly oiled and polished it; he had
put a newly-chipped flint in the hammer, and
when his companion struck the flint on the
empty pan (the sparks shone with a sudden
brilliancy in the gathering dusk) the lock
worked easily.

"I would try a little powder in it, Colin,"
suggested the younger lad.

"The night is so still they would hear it up
at Dunvorgan," said the elder lad, who was the
more prudent of the two.

"It will be giving no sound at all, Colin, if
there is no wadding in the barrel. You will
put a little powder in the barrel and a little
powder in the pan, and then you will see if the
little hole is all clear."

Well, there could be no objection to that, and
so Colin produced his precious canister and very
grudgingly measured out a few grains for the
experiment. The result was quite satisfactory.
There was a sharp click of the descending flint,
and almost at the same moment a flash of red
flame in the darkness. So the pistol was
carefully wrapped up in the old stocking that

was its customary case, and deposited in the locker along with the bottle of water and the oatmeal cakes which were their stores for the forthcoming voyage. Then the two lads got ashore again, and in the dusk made their way across the white sands and away up towards Dunvorgan farm.

For a time they were silent.

"I have been thinking, Archie," said the elder of the two, at last, " that it would not be a nice thing if the crew of the smack were to land and hunt us out. What would we do then ? "

The other made no reply.

"There would be five or six of them, Archie, and if they were to land, they would catch us, even if we were to go into the cave at the point opposite Rua. And if they were to catch us, Archie, it is not you and I that would be able to fight six of them."

And again, " I was thinking, Archie, that it would be better if I was to go by myself. It is not right that you should go into a risk for the sake of my father's sheep ; that is foolishness. I can manage the boat very well by myself."

" Then you can give me back my pistol,"

said the other, who was evidently deeply hurt. " If you think I am afraid, you can give me back my pistol."

" I did not say you were afraid.   I said there was a reason for my going, and there was no reason for your going.   If there was to be a fight, what would you do ? "

" What would you ?   Do you think that I am more afraid of the French fishermen than you ? Very well, then, I will take back my pistol."

Colin very soon perceived that his companion was bent on sharing this enterprise, whatever peril it might involve, and at last a compromise was effected ; Archie Livingston agreeing that in the event of the French fishermen venturing to land to discover who had fired at them, he should be the first to make for the little natural cave in the rocks that both the lads knew well, and that Colin should be allowed to look about a little and see what was likely to happen before seeking the same place of refuge.

It may be presumed that neither of the lads slept very much that night ; for besides the excitement of the enterprise, they had agreed to meet down at the little creek not later than half-past four in the morning.   And as each went stealthily his own way to the place of rendezvous, a fair still dawn was breaking over land and sea, and everything gave promise of a beautiful day. Moreover, the slight cool wind of the morning was blowing up from the south ; it was a fair wind to carry them out to the islands, where they were to lie in wait for the Frenchmen.

CHAPTER II.

THE setting forth of the two lads on their voyage to the far islands on the horizon was managed with all due secrecy and despatch, for both of them were well aware that if the people at the farm got to know on what mission they were bent they would immediately be stopped. But once away from the shore they grew more confident; and they could call to each other freely—Archie Livingston having been sent to the bow as a sort of look-out.

"Archie," called out the elder lad, who was at the stern, with the sheet of the mainsail in his hand and his elbow on the tiller, "they cannot stop us now."

"That they cannot, Colin."

"And do you think that Ailasa and Mary and the rest of them up at the shieling will be awake and out yet?"

"No doubt they will be awake and out," said

the younger lad—both of them speaking in Gaelic.

" For if any one is to see us they will be the first to see us, from the hillside. Yes, and maybe they are saying now, 'There is the boat going out; and who can be in the boat? and what does any one want to go to Farriskeir for?' Well, they will not be guessing that easily."

" Colin," said the younger lad, "it will be a hard thing if we have taken all this trouble and find none of the French fishermen coming near. I suppose you have heard that the French ships were always running away when they were told that Nelson was coming after them; and that it was not easy for him to fight them because he could not tell where they were ? Well, they are not running away from us ; but it will be just as bad if we do not find any of the smacks coming near Farriskeir or Rua-veg. And then what will you say when you go back ? "

" You are afraid of being laughed at," said the elder lad, "that is what I am thinking. You are afraid they will say, 'There are the boys who went out to frighten the Frenchmen and could not find them.' But answer me this,

Archie ; if we do not tell them why we went out, how will they know ? "

" If they have seen us from the shieling, Ailasa, or Red-haired Maggie, or one of them will be asking," said the other, diffidently.

" Yes, they will be asking ; it is the way of girls. But that is no need why we should tell. And this is what I am thinking of, Archie ; if there is not any French smack coming near the islands, well, we will go to the wreck, and there are many things that we can pick up ; and why should we not bring away a boatful of the spars and planks that my father drew above the water-mark at Rua ? It is very useful these things are at the farm ; and the last time we were out we had not an inch of spare room in the boat when we were coming back, such a load we had ; and if the girls at the shieling hear that we have brought back a cargo of wood from Rua-veg, what then ? Where will be their questions then ? "

They were now well away from the land ; and so steady was this light breeze from the south that the navigation of the boat involved no great care. The helmsman could with sufficient security turn from time to time to regard the

familiar landmarks they were leaving behind—
the wide white sands, the masses of rock, and
far beyond and above these the giant peaks of
Mealasabhal and Suainabhal all faintly coloured
by the morning sun. Or again, he would stand
up in the boat to get a better look at the islands
ahead ; and these, as the distance gradually grew
less, were beginning to show distinctive features
along their shores. But of any French smack or
other vessel they could find no sign whatever.
As far as their eyes could reach, this wide circle
of the blue Atlantic seemed to belong to them
selves. Once, indeed, they caught sight of the
topsails of a brigantine, the rest of the vessel
being below the horizon ; but apparently she
was beating down against the southerly breeze,
and, having put about, was soon lost to view.

" It will be no harm if we get out to the
islands without any one seeing us," said Colin
M'Calmont. " It will be a great deal better.
For if one of the smacks was to see us going
out, and if another smack was to take the word
to Reikjavik that there were people now on
Farriskeir and that they had guns, then there
would be a great laughing, and some of them
would be for saying, ' Why, are you frightened ?

It is no one but two boys who are on Farriskeir, for we saw them going out. And are you frightened because you heard the boys shooting at the curlews?'"

" That is true what you say, Colin; and anyway we will take back a load of wood with us," said the younger lad, who was very clearly anxious that the girls at the shieling should have no cause to jeer at them.

And now the islands grew more and more distinct; and as they drew nearer and nearer, the lads could see and hear that their appearance was causing a vast commotion among the innumerable wild-fowl that filled the air with their cries. The curlews uttered their warning whistle as they wheeled high in the air; the sea-pyots whirred along close to the water; the terns came flying overhead, screaming angrily as they dipped and rose again. And what was that great shapeless black thing, that lay on a spur of rock not nearly as large as itself?

" Colin," the younger lad cried, " look at that now! The wreck is not all gone away yet; and they were saying she would go to pieces before two days or three days were over, and not an inch would be left of her."

"There is not more than a third of her left now," Colin M'Calmont said; "and it is nothing but a lump of old iron she is. But we will go round the point of Rua and look at her. Slack the lee jib-sheet a bit, Archie; maybe we will get something out of her that may be of use at the farm."

"I would not go too near, Colin," said the younger of the two, "for she might tumble over on us."

"Tumble over on us!" said the other, with a laugh of derision. "When she has stood out two gales!"

But indeed when they rounded the point of one of the small islands and drew nearer to this great broken mass of iron perched high on a narrow ledge of rock, it was a gruesome sight, and they approached with caution. For one thing they had lowered their mainsail, and had taken to the oars, backing the stern of the boat towards the wreck (which towered high above them) so that they could see how near they could go in safety.

Huge as this rent and shattered fragment of a vessel seemed, the steamer had been of no great size; but when, on a pitch-dark night, and the

captain having made some mistake about the
lights along the coast, her stem was suddenly
jammed on to this rock, her impetus was great
enough to lift her up the shelving ledge, so that
at low water her keel forward was high and dry.
But her back was broken; and the first heavy
sea that came rolling in from the west knocked
her boilers out and tore down her stern into
deep water; leaving nothing standing but the
bow, which now presented an extraordinary
appearance.   Outside the hull was black, but
inside everything was red with rust; and as the
two lads backed their boat until this riven mass
of confusion seemed almost over their heads,
there was ·something awful in the evidence
everywhere around of the tremendous force of
the sea.   The twisted girders, the thick iron
plates, torn from their rivets and bent about as
if they had been made of pasteboard, the iron
cables snapped as if they had been so many
watch-chains—all this spoke of a frightful
combat; and seemed so strange, now, with this
placid blue sea all around, and all around, too, a
silence broken only by the distant calling of the
curlews.

The two lads regarded this picture of ruin and

desolation without uttering a word, apparently overawed by it; but at last Colin M'Calmont said,—

" Archie, do you not think I could climb up inside of her ? There might be something that one could find."

" Indeed you will get nothing but cut fingers with the broken iron," said Archie Livingston, with decision. " Did they not take everything out of her ? And what would you say now if one of the plates of iron were to fall on you ?"

The elder lad was still looking up, however, at the shattered remnant of the vessel.

"Archie, back her in a bit more ; and I will see if I can get up to the lower deck there."

The younger boy did as he was bid, though rather reluctantly ; and it was with a trifle of dismay that he beheld his companion clamber on to the wreck and begin to work his way up among the rusty iron. Then he saw him reach what remained of the lower deck, where there was still some woodwork ; and after searching about for a while he picked up something.

" Look there, Archie," he called out (his voice sounding hollow in the shell of the wreck), " I have found a pair of deer's horns. Take care, now, and I will throw them down to you."

The next moment the horns fell on the lowered mainsail and rebounded into the bottom of the boat.

"What is the use of them?" the younger lad cried—for he did not like the look of his companion clambering about up there. "If you want deer's horns, you will find them along the shore. It was part of her cargo. What is the use of deer's horns?"

However, something now happened that brought back Colin M'Calmont speedily enough into the boat, without any further remonstrance. In crossing over to the other side of this lower deck he found a place where he could look out to sea ; and of course at this height his view was far more extensive than that obtainable from the little sailing-boat below.

"I can see a big steamer away out there," he called, looking towards the west. "Where can she be going now? There is no steamer of that size will be going to Iceland."

The next minute, as he turned to the southern horizon, something caught his eye, which provoked no exclamation, but which caused him to hurry down from the wreck in half the time it had taken him to climb up.

"Archie," said he, in an excited whisper— although the boat he had seen was still miles off —"do you know this; there is a French smack coming up. I am sure of it—I know it—there is no other vessel that would be coming so near the land. Be quick now, Archie; we will row round to Farriskeir; I will not put the sail on her at all; we will row through the channel between Farriskeir and Rua, and maybe we will have her in the little harbour before they can see us. Do you understand that now?"

Archie Livingston took to his oar quickly enough, though, to tell the truth, he was somewhat alarmed. The adventure had been so far pleasant and romantic in its way; but it assumed a new aspect when he definitely knew that a crew of French fishermen were coming along, and probable danger at hand. He did not speak at all; and both knew equally well the course they had to make. They rowed away from the wreck; then along a narrow and tortuous channel between two islands; then they beheld before them the open sea again.

CHAPTER III.

"Do you see her?" said Colin M'Calmont, in the same low voice, as if the Frenchmen could hear at that distance.

"Yes," was the reply, as the younger lad descried the small dot of a vessel away down there in the south.

"Do you not think that is one of the smacks?"

"That is what I think." Then he added: "Colin, if they go by peaceably, and do not try to kill one of your father's sheep, we need not do anything? They will not know we are here."

"What did I come out for?" said the other, scornfully. "What did I come out for but to let every one of them know we are here? I want it talked about at Reikjavik; that is what I am thinking of. I do not wish to have any

more of my father's sheep killed. I wish them
to take the story to Reikjavik that there are
people on Farriskeir now, and that if any one
goes near to Farriskeir to have a shot at the
sheep—well, the shooting may not be all on one
side. It is not for nothing that I have come to
Farriskeir."

They rowed round the southern end of the
island, and then on the eastern side made their
way into a small naturally-formed harbour
which was protected by a low ridge of rock.
Over this rock the mast of the boat could be
seen easily enough; and that was what Colin
M'Calmont wanted. Even if the French fishermen did not approach the island, they would at
least see the mast of the boat (provided they
came that side) and would so gather that
Farriskeir was not always to be a happy
hunting-ground for them.

They got the anchor ashore, and made the
boat fast; then they had their own movements
to consider.

"Archie," said the elder, "if you are afraid,
go away to the cave at the end of the island;
they will never think of searching that."

"Whether I am afraid or not is no great

matter," said the other; "it is where you are that I am going to be."

"Oh, very well, then; we will now set about loading the pistol."

The pistol they had brought ashore with them; likewise the canister of powder, some wads, and a small paper bag full of shot.

"Are you going to put shot into it, Colin?" said the younger boy somewhat timidly, when his companion had filled in the powder and rammed the wad home.

"Well, now, it is much more than I that you will know about this pistol, Archie; but I was thinking if there were some shot put into it, it would make the greater noise, and be more like a gun. What do you say to that now?"

"But you will not fire at them?"

Colin M'Calmont laughed derisively—but not very loudly.

"And that is a very fine thing!" said he. "Who was it that wanted at the very beginning to have a shot at the Frenchmen? Who was it that was not afraid of the sheriff at Stornoway?"

"But it would be a dreadful thing to kill a man, Colin."

"Now that is the truth you are speaking, like

the old man of Ross. The old man of Ross
never said anything truer than that. And it is
not I that want to be taken before the sheriff at
Stornoway. No ; I am putting in shot to make
a fine good noise ; but afterwards I may also
put in shot ; do you see that now ? *This* time
it is to make a noise, and give them a story
to carry to Reikjavik ; *that* time it will be if
they want to land and chase us. And then
every one for himself ; that was what the weasel
said when he went home."

" Colin," said the younger lad, timidly, " when
we were coming near the island I saw two wild
swans fly away. It is not a good sign to see
the wild swans fly away from the island."

" Your head is full of nonsense," said the
other, scornfully.

" They say the wild swans are princesses,"
continued Archie Livingston, not heeding the
taunt, " that were changed by magic. And it is
not a good thing to see them fly away when you
come near the land."

" It is many and many a wild swan I have
seen—yes, thirty of them together, washing
themselves and flapping their wings in Loch-an-
Innis ; but never yet one that would wait till

you could put salt on its tail. Archie, my lad,
your head is full of nonsense. But if you are
afraid of wild swans, or princesses, or anything
else, then there is the cave for you; and you
can leave me to deal with the frog-eaters.
This is what I am afraid of; that they may not
come near enough—it is not the wild swans
that I am afraid of."

"And if I am afraid, I am not going to run
away," said his companion. "That is one thing
I am not going to do. Where you are, Colin, it
is there I am going to be."

"Very well, then, we will go and get a good
hiding-place behind the rocks; and you will be
very quiet, Archie, so that, if they think about
landing to steal a sheep, we will see it very
plainly; and then, after the shot, you will do as
I do—but not a word all the time."

It was not without a great deal of difficulty
and cautious experimenting that Colin M'Calmont found a suitable hiding-place for himself
and his companion. But at last he discovered
an abrupt little hollow behind a ledge of rock,
where, himself unseen, he could peep over and
watch the approach of the vessel that was now
drawing nearer and nearer; while, in the event

of the fishermen landing and pursuing them, they could from this point slip unperceived up to the northern end of the island, where there was a cave not likely to be discovered.

The smaller lad lay prone on the rock, motionless, scarcely daring to breathe. His companion from time to time cautiously peered over the edge; and now there was no doubt at all that the vessel was one of the French fishing-smacks bound for Iceland. M'Calmont took the precaution of putting a few grains of fresh powder in the pan of the pistol; then they waited—in a profound silence, broken only by the monotonous plashing of the sea along the rocks and the shingle.

Just in front of his head, as he lay on the sloping ledge of rock, M'Calmont had placed a few tufts of withered heather, through which he could easily see what was going on. And when the French vessel came along, and when he saw them deliberately put her head up to the wind, and lower a boat, and put two men in the boat, who calmly began to row to the island, his face grew red with anger. He dared not even whisper to his companion, who was lying mute and motionless beside him (and very much

D

afraid, too, though he would not have admitted it), and he was saying to himself,—

" If this now is not the most impudent thing ! Oh, yes, you will come and help yourself to a sheep—a sheep belonging to a poor man who has to work hard enough for his living; and you will have a good dinner on board, and a good laugh when you go to Iceland. It would take little now to make me fire at you and your boat, you French thieves ! "

But whether or no it was the fear of the sheriff at Stornoway, wiser counsels prevailed. When he had allowed the boat and the two men to come within thirty or forty yards of the island he took up the big horse-pistol and cocked the hammer. Then, holding it tight (for fear of the recoil) at arm's length from him, he pointed the pistol along the gully behind him, and pulled the trigger ; and the next second there was a sudden crash of noise in the silence, and a puff of splintered rock where the shot had struck.

Archie Livingston looked terrified; but M'Calmont, having serious work on hand, turned to his hiding-place again, and peeped through the tufts of heather to see what effect this shot might have had.

The men in the boat were very obviously surprised. They had stopped rowing. One of them, indeed, was now standing up, closely scanning the shore ; and M'Calmont kept himself closely concealed, for he knew that the smoke from the gunpowder would give them some more or less vague indication of his whereabouts.

What would they do ? Would they go back to the fishing-smack, merely with the impression that now there were people living on the island ? Or would they consider that they had been fired at, and be tempted to make reprisals ?

He could see that they were excitedly talking to each other ; and one of them pointed to the little creek in which M'Calmont's sailing-boat lay ; then they put their oars into the water again, and continued rowing for the shore.

"They are going to land, Archie!" said M'Calmont, in a quick whisper. "Come along —sharp! We will make for the cave ; and there will be time to load the pistol there. Quick! quick, now! and keep low down."

But every nook and gully of the island was well known to both of them ; and they easily made their way to the north end of the island without showing themselves on any of the little grassy plateaus or of the higher rocks. Fortunately, too, for them, their appearance earlier in the day had frightened the half-wild sheep over to the western side of the island, so that there was no scurrying of startled animals to show their track.

They reached the coast-line again ; made their way along some rocks ; and then slipping down cautiously, entered a small cave that just allowed them to stand upright. The floor was of sand and shells washed in by the high tides ; a few tufts of sea-asplenium showed their dark-green fronds in the shelves and crannies ; otherwise the cave was pretty much of a bare, black hole, with a curious damp odour of sea-weed in it.

"Now, Archie, the powder—quick ! "—for the younger lad had charge of the ammunition.

It cannot be denied that Archie's fingers were trembling somewhat as he produced the tin canister ; but his companion did not notice that —he was too anxious to have the pistol loaded. And when that was completed he seemed to breathe more freely.

"Now do you see this, Archie," said he,

cheerfully, " that we have the best of the position ? For if they come after us and find out the cave, we are in the dark, and they cannot make us out, but they are in the light, and we will see everything they mean to do. And there are only two of them ; and what I am determined on is this—if they try to do any harm to us, I will put a shot on to them, whether there is a sheriff in Stornoway or no. It is no use speaking to them, for they do not understand any language but their own. And if they point a gun at you or me, it is I that will be firing first, or you may call me a splay-footed* fellow. But as for you, Archie, if they find out the cave, you will go right to the back of the cave, and you will lie down, with your face to the ground, and they will not see you at all. For it is better to be safe without fighting than to be safe after fighting, as the old man of Ross said."

They waited and waited, and there was not a sound outside.

" I wonder now," the elder lad said at length,

* *Guagaire* was the word he used, but, besides meaning "splay-footed," it is also used to denote one who is idle or giddy or frivolous.

" whether they thought I was firing the shot at
them ? Perhaps they did not come ashore at
all. That will be much better; if they have
gone back to the others, and told them that
the time is past now for having a sheep off
Farriskeir."

" I am sure I hope they have gone away,
Colin," said the younger of the boys, who had
not spoken since they entered the cave.

He had been listening for sounds without, not
quite certain whether, in the event of pursuit,
he should take his companion's advice and hide,
or whether he ought not to lend what help he
could.

Suddenly something occurred that made both
the lads start. They found two eyes glaring
into the cave—two large, soft, staring eyes, that
belonged to a bushy, flat-shaped head ; and then
the next moment, before they had time to recover from their fright, the strange creature had
turned and made off as quickly as its webbed
feet and long tail would allow.

" Well, I never saw an otter on the land
before," said Colin M'Calmont, who was the first
to recover his presence of mind. " He must
have come up through the sea-weed there. If

it was not for the Frenchmen, maybe I could
catch him yet; for they go very slow on the
land."

" Colin, do not go out of the cave," the other
entreated. " As for the otter, what is an otter?
You can trap one at Camus Head if you want
one. And as for that one, he is down through
the sea-weed and into the sea long ago. He
will be as far away as Rua-veg by this time."

Nevertheless, with the natural curiosity of a
young lad, Colin must needs go to the mouth of
the cave, and peer cautiously around. There
was no sign of any otter, and there was neither
sign nor sound of the French fishermen. But
the next second something else caught his eye.

" Archie, come here!" he called out. " Come
here, now! See, the smack is away to the
north. I know that is the same one from the
red patch on her mainsail. They have gone
away now, Archie."

" And a good thing, too," said the younger
lad, coming out to the light and the warmer air.
" Yes, that is the smack, Colin, I believe. And
now they will take the story to Reikjavik."

" Yes," said his companion, with something of
triumph in his face and tone. " That is true.

And there will be no more stealing of the sheep now. And what we have to do now is to put some of the timber and the spars into the boat, and get away back to the mainland. And you will not be afraid of the questions any more, Archie, if the girls at the shieling will be asking you why you went to Farriskeir. For did we not prevent the Frenchmen landing? And we have saved one, or maybe more, of my father's sheep; and the warning to the frog-eaters will be a good thing besides. There is only the one thing now that I am sorry for."

"And what is that, Colin?"

"That I did not have a shot at the otter."

"That am I not sorry for," said his friend (who had regained all his modest confidence and cheerfulness), "it was a more important thing than an otter that we came for; and never before did I hear my pistol make such a noise."

"I thought my arm was off," said Colin, with a laugh.

They had by this time got back to the gully behind the ledge of rock which they had chosen for their hiding - place; and some distance beyond that again was the creek where they had moored their sailing-boat. All at once

M'Calmont paused with a strange look on his face.

"Archie, where is the boat?" said he.

The younger lad glanced at him awe-stricken. It was more from the look of Colin's face than from anything else that he guessed something was wrong.

◆ "Archie, they've stolen the boat—they've taken away the boat!" said the elder lad, gazing at the empty creek.

"That is not possible, Colin," said the other (but with a sudden sinking of the heart). "They dare not do that. It would be seen. They had no boat towing astern. Maybe they have hid it, Colin, for a joke."

Without answering Colin ran up to the top of one of the higher plateaus, and eagerly scanned every little indentation of the coast-line. But no mast was visible; and the mast of the boat was higher than any of these rocks. Then his quick eye noticed something floating on the water some forty or fifty yards out, and then something else—a basket that he recognised; and then he knew what had happened.

CHAPTER IV.

BUT before going down to his companion he pulled himself together. He knew that Archie Livingston was easily frightened; and this that had happened was enough to frighten an older lad than he. M'Calmont descended from the plateau slowly, considering what he should say, and doing his best to assume an indifferent demeanour.

"Archie," said he, "there is no doubt about what the Frenchmen have done. They have taken out the boat and sunk her. Yonder are things belonging to her, floating on the water; but not the oars. They have stolen the oars."

Almost mechanically the younger lad's eyes were turned to the space of water indicated by his companion; then he said, aghast,—

"Colin, we shall die of hunger."

Colin had been prepared for this.

"Die of hunger!" he exclaimed. "Now you

are talking like some poor creature who has never been away from a town. You are talking like the tailor who came to Bernera last year, and he did not know that cattle could swim."

"How could we swim to the mainland?" said the younger lad, who seemed ready to cry. "It is twelve miles and more."

"I did not mean that at all. I say you are talking foolishness when you speak of dying of starvation; and that you ought to know better, being a Highland lad, and not a tailor from Glasgow."

Indeed, this raising of his companion's spirits was giving M'Calmont himself plenty of spirits.

"Now look here, Archie. The loss of the boat, that is bad; my father can ill afford to lose the boat, and that is a hard thing. But there is no more than that. They will soon find out that we are here, and they will send over for us; and until they send over for us, do you not think we will find enough and plenty to eat? Is there no dulse along the shore? Are there no *eachans** in the sand? One would think, to

* The *eachan* is a shell-fish resembling the cockle, but a trifle smaller, and with a smooth shell. It is similar to, if it

hear you talk, that you were the high Lord
Provost of London, who eats all the day long
and half-way through the night, and only stops
to sleep for an hour or two. Tell me this, now ;
if eachans and dulse will not do, if it is to be
like the Lord Provost you are wishing, could I
not shoot a sheep ? Just think of that ; and do
not talk any more about starvation."

"But how will they know that we are here,
Colin ? " said the younger lad, looking far away
over to the blue line, with one or two higher
peaks, that represented the mainland.

"I will tell you a story, Archie. It was a
fishing-boat at St. Kilda, and she went away in
the morning, with five men in her, and there
was a heavy storm during the day, and the boat
was smashed on a small island—perhaps it was
Eilean Môr and perhaps it was Gealtaire Môr ;
that is no matter ; but the five men saved themselves. Very well, then ; what did they do ?
They gathered bits of stick, and dried heather,
and the like, and they made them into five

---

is not identical with, the American clam ; and it is odd that,
while it is the common shell-fish of the sandy bays in the
western Highlands, it is quite unknown, as far as I am
aware, in the south of Great Britain.

fires ; and when the night came they lit the five fires, and their wives and the people at St. Kilda saw the fires, and they knew that all the men were saved. Now, does that story tell you anything, or does it not tell you anything ? "

" We will light a fire to-night, Colin ! " said the younger lad, eagerly.

" We will not. What would be the use of that ? They will not be looking out for us at all ; for they will think that we have gone away up to the shieling with bread for the girls. But to-morrow the girls will be sending down ; and then they will ask where we are ; and then there will be a search everywhere ; and then in the evening we will have a great heap of wood together and the dried heather too ; and they will see the fire well enough."

" Will we have to stay on the island to-night, Colin ? " said Archie, looking apprehensively around—for his mind was stocked with the mysterious legendary tales and fancies of these northern solitudes.

" I do not say that, Archie," replied his companion, grimly. " If you can swim to the mainland, there will be no need to pass the night on Farriskeir. But if you can, it is not I that can.

It is a good swim from Farriskeir to the White Sands of Uig."

And then he looked out at the one or two objects floating in the water which told him where the Frenchmen had sunk the boat.

"Yes," said he, "and they have sunk our oat-cake, too, and our bottle of water. I know where there are two springs, but the sheep tread over them, and if we clean them out, it will be a long time before they settle. So we will do that first, Archie. You will clean out the springs, and I will go to the wreckage that my father and the rest of them collected, and I will get two or three boards and put over the springs so that the sheep may not trample over them."

The first spring they went to looked un-promising enough; it was more like a patch of green mire in a hollow of one of the grassy plateaus. But they sought out its source, and the younger lad set to work to remove the muddy herbage, while his companion went away for two or three planks.

Indeed, they had plenty of work cut out for themselves during the day. They hunted for dulse. They each got a piece of iron from off the wreckage and dug in the soft sand for eachans. And then they gathered bracken for their bedding; whereupon arose the question as to where they should pass the night.

"The driest place would be the cave," said Colin, "and you will see by the withered sea-weed on the shore that it is many a day since the sea washed any sand into the cave. There is no danger of that at all. It is with a spring tide and a heavy gale from the west that you might have water in the cave." ˙

"Colin," said the other, doubtfully, "I have heard about wild cats being about the caves."

"There is not a wild cat on the island," said the other, impatiently. "Do you think that wild cats can swim from the mainland? It is all very well for an otter to swim from the mainland, and if an otter comes into the cave, who will be the more frightened? It is not you or I, but the otter, that will get a fright if he comes in the night-time and finds us there asleep. And this is what I am thinking of now, Archie; will we not take some of the planks into the cave, and put them on the sand, and put the bracken on them? and that will make a very good bed indeed. Oh, we will do very

well. You know what they say; when you
cannot get a deer of ten* be satisfied with a
deer of eight."

He was a shifty lad; and when the two companions that night, having had their supper of
cachans, with a good drink of clear spring water,
went and lay down on a comfortable bed of
bracken made up within the cave, they could
not be considered to be very badly off.

But what chiefly exercised Colin M'Calmont's
mind (though he said nothing about it to Archie)
was as to the way in which his father would
receive the news of the loss of the boat. Would
he take into consideration his son's good inten-
tions? Or would he jump to the conclusion
that he had lost this valuable piece of property
simply through an inexcusable outburst of
boyish folly? It was a serious question; for
old M'Calmont was a strict disciplinarian. In
the meantime Colin had but little doubt about
himself and his companion being able to get
back to the mainland—when once they had had
a great bonfire lit on the highest point of Farriskeir.

The gray dawn broke.   ,

* Of ten points—referring to the antlers.

"Colin," said the younger lad, who had not slept much, " did you hear the strange sounds in the night?"

" No, I heard no sounds at all," said his companion drowsily.

"There were cries and strange noises; I do not wish to have another night on the island."

" It is your head that is full of nonsense; and you were hearing the sea-pyots and curlews. Now I am going to sleep again."

"I cannot sleep any more," the younger lad said. "Now that there is daylight I am going to the spring for a drink of fresh water."

Colin M'Calmont turned himself over on his bed of bracken; and the younger lad wandered out into the silence and solitude of the early morning.

Very soon M'Calmont was asleep again. He was not an over-imaginative person; he did not bother his head about dreams and portents; and besides, they had been very early up on the previous morning. The bed of bracken was soft enough, and there was no sound to break the silence save the drowsy murmur of the sea outside. He was fast asleep.

But suddenly he found himself wakened

E

again ; and he became dimly aware that Archie Livingston had a tight grip of his arm and was kneeling beside him. He roused himself. He found that his companion was all trembling ; and that he could scarcely speak.

" What is it, Archie ? " he said.

" I—I have seen one of them," the younger boy gasped, and still he clung to his companion's arm as if for safety. " Oh, Colin, it is a terrible sight ! Quite plain—down by the rocks—it did not move——"

Colin sat up and rubbed his eyes.

" What is this now ? " said he, with a trifle of impatience.

" It is no foolishness this time," the younger lad said, almost entreatingly. " You will see for yourself, Colin, if you have the courage to go. It is like a woman. It is one of the princesses. But she did not see me ; or she would have changed into a swan and flown away. But it was a terrible, terrible sight ; I will never forget it till the day I die——"

" I tell you, Archie," said the other, angrily, " that if you let such nonsense come into your head, it is mad you will be in time. Come and let me see your princesses and your wild swans now! And if it is a wild swan, perhaps I will tickle him before he flies away."

He got up and sought out the horse-pistol, which he had put in a dry place.

" Come away, now, and let me see your wild swan that is like a princess."

" Oh no, I cannot! I cannot, Colin!" said the younger lad, who was still trembling.

" But I say you must now. I will put the nonsense out of your head. Do you wish to become mad, and go through the villages like Alister, the piper's son, that the children make a fool of ? "

And then he took to the ironical method.

" Do you know this now, Archie, that I never heard of the ghost yet that would stand to have a charge of buck-shot put into it. It will be very fine now to have a shot at a ghost. Come away, Archie; and if we meet any ghost or princess or anybody of that kind, it is I who will go forward and speak to them and say, ' Good morning.' For that is good manners to a stranger; and my father has the farming of Farriskeir; and if a stranger comes to Farriskeir, it is not I that would be so unfriendly as not to say ' Good morning.' "

It was with the greatest reluctance that

E 2

Archie Livingston consented to go out from the cave again with his companion; and when at last he undertook to show M'Calmont where he had seen this strange thing he advanced with stealthy step and bated breath. Of course M'Calmont did not expect to see anything. It was to cure the imagination of the boy that he had insisted on going to the spot. And therefore he went on unheeding, chiefly watching the wild birds that were flying about.

At a certain eminence on one of the little plateaus, Archie Livingston gripped his arm, and he stopped to ask what this meant; but at the same moment he caught sight of something down by the shore there that—despite all his determination—made his face turn perfectly white. He would not budge. He stood still; but he found himself incapable of speaking.

There, sure enough, down near the water's edge and seated on a rock, was a figure. It could not be an optical illusion; for they were both regarding the same spot. And it was the figure of a woman, too—bent forward, her face resting on her hands and covered. And this woman was not dressed as any person in the Highlands dressed.

He stood and stared; trying to get the better of this thumping of his heart, and summoning to his aid all his declared disbelief in ghosts. Then the woman down there lifted her head—wearily, as it seemed to him; then she caught sight of the lads, and sprang to her feet with a slight cry, and advanced to them—her hands stretched out before her, and she was saying something. Now when she made this sudden and quick advance, Colin M'Calmont, despite himself, retreated a couple of steps; but he kept his face towards her; and then he stood.

CHAPTER V.

"Archie," said Colin, in a low voice, "it is a woman. It is not any ghost. I cannot make out what she says except '*peety, peety!*'"

The young woman came nearer to them—now timidly and slowly—her hands still outstretched, and tears running down her face, while she spoke rapidly and imploringly. This appeal, which was a mute appeal so far as he was concerned, drove any remnant of fear out of his mind; he forgot even his timid companion behind; he went forward to her, wondering how he could convey to this poor young lady that they wished to be very friendly to her.

He shook his head, to let her know he did not understand her; and then she, with a great deal more of gladness in her face—for she could not but see that the lads wished to be friendly— began to try to explain her situation by signs. And again and again she pointed to the north, though there was no boat visible.

"Colin," said the younger lad, "she has been going to Iceland in one of the smacks; and the smack has got wrecked, and she has been saved."

"How could that be? Her clothes have not been in the water."

"Colin, say *France* to her, and you will see if she is French."

Colin repeated this word to her, which, to tell the truth, was all of the French language that either he or his companion knew; and instantly the young lady nodded eagerly, and said something which, of course, they did not understand.

And now that they had begun to communicate with each other by signs it soon became clear that the younger lad was much sharper at that than his companion. In fact, Archie Livingston became the interpreter.

"When she means 'yes,'" said he, to his companion, "sometimes she says *see* and sometimes *wee;* but a nod of the head is still surer. And she says she will go with us to the mainland; but how am I to tell her that we have no boat, and that she must wait till the evening before we can light the bonfire?"

"Well, you must get on as well as you can,

Archie," said the other; " and there is the whole
day for you to talk to her with your head and
your hands ; and in the meanwhile I am going
away to dig for *eachans*, for who knows when the
lady may have had anything to eat ? "

" Do you think she will eat *eachans?* " said
Archie, doubtfully."

" It is better to eat *eachans* than to starve,"
said the other.   " You do not need the old man
of Ross to tell you that.   And if she is from
France, people who eat frogs need not turn up
their noses at *eachans*."

In not much more than a quarter of an hour
Colin M'Calmont returned, carrying in both
hands a sort of basket made of the fronds of the
bracken, and in this green nest lay a quantity of
eachans, like so many eggs, all washed white and
clean.   He put them down in front of her, and
took out his pocket-knife and opened a few, as
one might open oysters ; and these he offered to
her.   What she did was singular.   She took his
hand and pressed it, and then smiled and shook
her head.

" Perhaps see is not hungry," Colin said, after
a second.

" Perhaps she does not like shell-fish raw,"

said the other. " Could you not roast some,
Colin, as the mussels are roasted ? Could we
not make a small fire now, and roast some
eachans in the ashes ? "

" I see no difficulty about that whatever."

Nor was there. He collected some tufts of
withered heather, and broke up one or two
pieces of wood, and put underneath the pile a
piece of a copy of the *Oban Times* that he had
brought with him for wadding ; and at the edge
of the paper placed a small *pioye.* The flint
from the horse-pistol and the back of his knife
did the rest, and soon they had a small fire
burning—the precursor of the greater bonfire of
the evening.

When the *eachans* were roasted Colin carefully
picked out some of them from the ashes with a
bit of stick ; and Archie, when they were sufficiently cool to be touched, brought them along
and offered them to the lady. Tears came into
her eyes as he did so. He thought it very
strange that any one should cry for no apparent
reason ; but he was glad to see that she took
one or two of the roasted shell-fish.

" I am thinking," said the elder of the lads,
" that she is only taking them to please us.

If she was hungry, she would be quicker. I
wonder now if it is not a drink of water she
would rather have than anything else? These
French people are very unfortunate that they
speak such a language."

But Archie Livingston, taking the hint, went
away along the shore, kicking the sea-weed
about until he found a large scallop shell, which
he washed free of sand in the nearest pool.
Then he went away over the grassy hillocks till
he came to the spring, where he filled the shell.
To carry anything like the full quantity back
was clearly impossible; but at least there was
enough to let her understand that there was
fresh water on the island.

And how grateful the young lady seemed!
She patted the boy on the head—on the
shoulder—on the hand. And she spoke to him,
though she knew he could not comprehend what
she said.

"But did you hear that, Colin?" he said,
turning to his companion. "She said a great
deal about mercy.' She said the water was a
mercy. Now, that is what they say also in
English; when you have your food put before
you—the meat and the drink—and when you

do not ask the blessing in Gaelic, then you have
to call these things on the table 'mercies.' She
must be very well brought up, and not a
heathen at all."

"But this is what I am thinking of, Archie,"
said the other; "that the little water you can
get in a scallop shell is not of much use to any
one. And if I could understand the lady as well
as you can, I would ask her to go with me to the
spring, and there she can have as much water as
she likes."

When this proposal was conveyed to her, she
followed her guide gladly, and when they
reached the spring she drank of the water freely
by means of this shell. And then they went
back to the fire, where Colin M'Calmont was
having his breakfast; and the young lady made
signs to the younger lad that he, too, was to
join in that feast of roasted *eachans*, and that
she was quite content.

"Well, this is a strange thing," said the
younger one; "but when we get back to the
mainland we will know all about it, for my
father knows French as well as Latin and a great
many other things."

"But what is the use of knowing French?"

said the elder lad, who was a practical youth, and better acquainted with the price of sheep.

"The use of it? The use of it is to make you a learned person, and then the people pay you for teaching others."

"But your father does not teach any one French, Archie."

"Well, then, the use of it is to make you not so ignorant as the other common people. When Sir Evan Roy comes to Glen Estera he will be speaking quite freely with my father; but the other ones they have to think about their English."

"I think Gaelic is as good a language as any; and also that it is more easily spoken than any other."

"But of what use to you is Gaelic if you go away from the Lewis? For my part, I would like to know six or seven languages."

"That would be a fine thing!" said the other, with a laugh of scorn. "To spend all your life in learning the languages of other people; and then, when you had got them, it would be time to die. I think one language is quite enough for any one; and Gaelic is the easiest."

When they had finished their breakfast, they

also went and had a drink of fresh water; and
then they set to work to carry up to the highest
plateau a pile of the wood that plentifully be-
strewed the western shores of the island—some
of it, indeed, having been hauled up above high-
water mark for transportation to the mainland. The steamer had been comparatively a
new one, and much of this wreckage consisted of
internal fittings—cabin doors and tables, bottle
ranges, benches, lockers, and what not—that
had been wofully smashed.

"It is very hard to burn all this good wood,"
said Colin M'Calmont; "and much of it ma-
hogany, too ; but we must have a big blaze, and
then we are saving the lady's life."

"Yes, and our own lives too," said the
younger lad, sitting down for a rest, for it was
stiff work carrying these planks. "They will
not be mourning over the wood when they find
us alive. And by this time now, Colin, by this
time, do you not think some one of the girls
must have been sent down from the shieling for
bread ? "

" By this time, surely."

"Then they will know we were not at the
shieling last night, and they will be looking

everywhere for us; and they will be sure to go and look if the boat is in the creek. And when they see that the boat is not in the creek, they will know how we went away; and you may be sure there will be many a sharp eye on the look-out all the day and all the evening."

"Very well, now, Archie, I will tell you what you will do. You will leave the rest of the building of the bonfire to me, for I am not easily tired; and you will go back and talk to the lady with your hands and your head as you were doing. Perhaps I will not use any more of the wood; that is the thing that is grieving me. I will build up three or four feet of the withered heather, and then I will put the wood on that. If it was only the autumn now, and we could get the withered bracken, there would be no need to use all that fine wood."

"Have you a lead pencil, Colin?"

"I have a small bit."

Archie was at this moment rummaging among the splinters and boards they had brought up; and at last he lit upon a piece of wood, painted white, that had been part of the door of a locker.

"Give me your pencil, Colin, and I will go and tell the lady what we are waiting for."

"And if you cannot speak French, are you going to be writing French?" said the other, with a laugh.

"I am not going to write at all, Colin, except in the way that the ancient people wrote, on the Pyramids and such places as that. And you will see whether the lady will understand or whether she will not understand."

"Very well, then, Archie; go back to the lady, and I will go on with the bonfire; and this is what I am thinking, that I will build a bonfire that will be easily made out from the land. For you know what they say: '*There cannot be anything in the sky or on the earth, but the Islay men's eyes can behold; nor can anything in a corner or lockfast place escape the eye of a Mullman.*' But what I say is that the Lewis men have sharper eyes than either."

"I think every one knows that," said Archie, "from Fraserburgh all the way round to Greenock."

Well, when M'Calmont had finished piling up this great heap of heather and driftwood, he went and rejoined his companion; and found, to his great astonishment, that the young lady—whose black eyes seemed to be full of gladness

and kindness and gratitude—appeared to understand the whole situation of affairs. For young
Livingston had drawn various things, in a rude
sort of way, on the bit of white wood ; and she
seemed a clever, imaginative sort of person, for
she guessed eagerly what he meant to convey.

"I never saw a boat like that, Archie," said
the elder lad, laughing, "for you have got the
mast in the middle of her."

"That is no matter at all," said the other,
without confusion, "if the lady understands that
the boat will come for her after the bonfire
is lit."

"Then you might be doing a worse thing
than asking her to come and look at the bonfire,
now that it is complete. I can tell you, Archie,
that my arms will be sore to-morrow."

The boy showed her the rough sketch of a
bonfire that he had made on the board, and
then pointed to the middle of the island, himself setting out, and inviting her to accompany
him. She understood at once, and smilingly
assented. They led her by the driest ways (for
there was some mossy ground on these plateaus)
to the spot, and she seemed greatly pleased.

"She can speak a little, Archie," said the

elder one. "It is not much; but it is a little. She cannot say ' bonfire,' but she says ' bon, bon ' —which is a part of it. Though she speaks through her nose, she understands well enough. The French are not so stupid as people say."

They passed the afternoon somehow. More cachans were roasted. As the evening fell the southerly wind freshened, and the skies got darkened over.

" I hope there is not going to be a gale," said the younger lad, apprehensively.

" That is not any gale," said the other. " And if there was a gale now? We should be two or three days more on the island, perhaps; and what is that? Maybe I would have to shoot a sheep; for the finely brought up people they cannot live on a handful of cachans and a bit of dulse as you or I could, Archie. But that is not any gale; and the darker it grows the sooner will we light the bonfire; and the fresher the wind the sooner will the people come across in your father's boat. So there is nothing to have a downcast face about; and you must not show a downcast face; for the lady there she watches us both, and every one knows that women are easily frightened persons."

F

They waited until the dusky twilight had gathered over land and sea before they lit the bonfire. At first there was only a little crackling ; then a few thin red tongues of fire ; then a growing blaze of crimson and orange that made the surrounding twilight look a strange, intense, livid blue. And then the fire began to roar, for the breeze fanned it; and soon there was a blazing mass of flame that surely would carry a message to the distant shores of Lewis.

"Archie," said the elder lad, "you will keep stirring the bonfire now, and I will go for another armful or two of wood. We must have a big blaze in case there might be a shower of rain. Yes ; and if there are any French smacks going by in the night, do you not think now that such a blaze as that will tell them that there is some one on Farriskeir?"

He went and came back with the first load of the driftwood.

"The sheep are wild with fright, Archie ; they never saw anything like this on Farriskeir before."

He fetched another load.

"There, now," said he, "that will make a

blaze that will be seen from Gallon Head to Scarfa Island. And if they are already in your father's boat, it is not I that would be surprised; and with a good breeze of wind like this they will not be long in coming over."

" Colin," said the younger lad, " this is what I am thinking of; when your father, or my father, or perhaps Dugald M'Lean from Glen Estera, comes over in the boat, and they will ask about the lady there, and who she is, and where she came from, what is it now that we will be saying ? "

Colin laughed, in his superior wisdom.

"Then you do not remember what the old man of Ross said. This is what he said, Archie : ' *That which you do not know, tell that to no one.*' How are we to be answering anything about the French young lady ? Let them ask for themselves. And indeed I wish they were here ; for it is not a pleasant thing that you and I should be talking and talking, and the lady there not able to know what is going on, because she understands nothing but that useless language. And if your father can speak that language, it is not anything to be proud of. He might have made a better use of his time."

F 2

The younger lad thought over this for some time. Then he said,—

"Well, perhaps the French is not a very useful language while you are in the Lewis or any other part of that country. But if you wished to go to France? If you wished to go to France, Colin, you would have to learn it. There now."

"If I wished to go to France!" said the other, scornfully. "And who would be so foolish as that? There is another wish that I have, that has more of common-sense in it. I would like to go to Fraserburgh, and see the great fleet of fishing-boats. Now there would be some sense in that."

CHAPTER VI.

THEY formed a picturesque group there on the summit of the level plateau—the smaller lad stirring up the smouldering portions of the bonfire, the elder heaping on broken planks and sticks, the young girl standing apart and sometimes watching them and sometimes scanning the now darkened plain of the waters whence she understood that help was to come ; while as the masses of roaring fire waxed or waned, the long black shadows moved on the greensward and the rocks.

Perhaps, indeed, it was their tending of the bonfire that prevented the lads from keeping a sharp look-out ; at all events it was neither of them that first discovered that people were coming to their rescue. They had had the bonfire blazing for nearly an hour, when suddenly the young lady came to them and eagerly said something, and pointed towards the sea in the direction of the mainland.

Both of the lads withdrew from the glare of the bonfire and peered into the darkness with eyes that were well accustomed to descry distant objects.

"Well, now," said Colin M'Calmont, with some mortification, "it will be a strange thing if a French lady can make out what I cannot make out; but there is not anything that I can make out between here and the land."

"Your eyes are blind with the fire, Colin, and so are mine," said his companion. "I wish I could ask her what it is."

"I see it! I see it! it is a light!" exclaimed M'Calmont, with involuntary eagerness. Then he immediately checked himself. Throughout he had spoken as if their rescue was a matter of course in order to keep up his companion's spirits. He was not going to betray any extraordinary surprise, or delight, or thankfulness now. So he continued in a tone of cool criticism,—

"Well, now, Archie, that is a strange sort of light. Your father has a lantern for the dark nights; but that is not a lantern at the masthead at all. It is very low down, and it is red."

"Maybe it is a torch at the bow," suggested Archie Livingston.

"And you will be making a very good guess that time, Archie, for now I can see the sparks ; and the sparks are dropping like sparks from a squib. Oh, this is a fine breeze, to be sure ; and your father's boat is as quick a sailer as any one on the west coast of the Lewis. I should not wonder if they could hear us now."

Herewith he gave a tremendous long, slow howl, such as the shepherds use when the dogs are far up on the hill. But there was no response.

"They will be too far away yet," said his companion. "Indeed, Colin, it is not I that am sorry we have not to stay another night on the island. It was terrible—the cries——"

"They were the cries of the French lady, that was all," said the elder lad. "To think they were the cries of ghosts ! Tell me this, Archie ; if you can see through a ghost, and if a ghost can go away into nothing, where is the throat for it to make a cry with ? It is your head that is full of nonsense about ghosts and things like that. This is what I will do for you now,

Archie; you will catch one of your ghosts and
bring him to me; and I will take the knife I
have for opening the mussels for bait, and I will
cut open the ghost for you, and then you will be
seeing whether he has any lungs, or a throat, or
a tongue that could make a noise. I tell you I
have not as much fear of a ghost as I have of a
skate. When you are cutting open a skate,
sometimes he will snap at your finger. I will
let the ghost snap at my finger if he can."

Whether this logic quite convinced Archie
Livingston is not of much moment; he merely
said, "It is I who am glad not to have another
night on Farriskeir," and kept his eyes fixed
on the sputtering red light that was now
momentarily ·coming nearer.

What a wild torrent of Gaelic was poured
forth when the farmer and the schoolmaster got
ashore—Colin and Archie helping to haul the
bow of the boat up on to the shingle! Indeed,
amid all these questions and exclamations and
remonstrances the worthy schoolmaster quite
forgot that ordinarily he made it a strict rule to
speak only in English. How could English—
which is a slow, formal, limited language—have
got from the boys a narration of all their

adventures during these past two days? But
that over, Mr. Livingston recollected himself.

"Archie," said he, in his best English, "you
wass saying the leddy is a French leddy!"

"*Seadh!*" said Archie; and then he too,
recollected himself. "Ay, she's French. And
no word of English at ahl."

"Kott pless me!" said the schoolmaster,
looking somewhat distressed. And then he
turned to his friend M'Calmont, Colin's father.

"It is a terriple pusiness," said he, "to speak
in another langwich when one is not speaking it
for many years and years. Heh, Duncan, gif
me the oat-cake and the whiskey out of the
locker; and be quick about it, too. The boys
are goot boys, and do not touch the whiskey;
but if the young leddy has had nothing to eat
ahl the day but *eachans*, she will hef a drop
of whiskey and no harm whateffer. And
whiskey is a goot langwich that every one can
understand."

The young French lady had come down from
the plateau, and was standing apart—observing
everything eagerly, but not attempting to speak.
She could see by their gestures and by their
occasionally looking towards her, that they were

telling the story, so far as they knew it. But presently Mr. Livingston, having got some whiskey in a tumbler, and carrying a piece of oat-cake in his other hand, went along to where she was standing and made her a most gracious and courteous bow.

Then he considered. He looked at her dark eyes vaguely (everything was lit up by the glare from the bonfire), as if he was wondering how to open communication with her. Then he said, slowly,—

" Mademoiselle—*ici est—est* oat-cake—*et aussi* whiskey—*très bon pour vous*——"

But at the same instant he was evidently startled by her uttering a slight cry—partly of delight, partly of entreaty ; and the next moment she was pouring out the story of her wrongs and griefs, with many piteous gestures and appeals.

The schoolmaster was quite bewildered. She spoke so rapidly, so pathetically, that he did not understand a single word ; he could only vaguely gather from her piteous intonation that she had suffered injury and was begging him to be kind to her.

" Kott pless me ! Kott pless me !" he mur-

mured to himself; "it is a terrible thing to understand a stranche langwich. The poor creature! She will pay no heed to the oat-cake and the whiskey."

Then to add to his confusion the farmer came up.

"Well, now, Mr. Livingston, and what iss the matter about the young leddy? It is the stranchest thing I ever heard of. How wass she come to Farriskeir?"

"You will see this, Dunvorgan,"* said the schoolmaster, "the French langwich is not like other langwiches; when it iss spoke slow, then effery one will understand it that knows it: but when it iss spoke quick, then no one understands it at ahl. We will get the young leddy into the poat, and we will tek her back home with us; and maype on the way I will hef the story to tell to you."

When the young lady understood that she was to go into the boat, she obeyed willingly; and when she had taken her seat in the stern, there was handed to her a rug made of the very finest sheep's wool, that Archie Livingston's mother

---

* The name of the farm. These territorial designations are common in Scotland.

had sent, thinking that the boys might have
been shipwrecked and be found on the rocks
with wet clothes.   But indeed the night was not
cold, and she merely let the rug lie across her
knees.   She seemed to care about nothing but
having her story understood by the only one
among these friendly people who knew a little of
French.

And when at length they had got the boat
afloat again, and the mainsail hoisted, and when,
in the silence of the night, they proceeded to
make their way back to the mainland of Lewis,
the schoolmaster managed to hint to her that, if
she would speak slowly, and say what she had
said all over again, he would understand her
better.   This intimation she seemed to comprehend very well; for now she began very
patiently to speak to him; and she instantly
paused when he seemed not to follow her, so
that he might have time to repeat the word or
to question her.

"Pless me, Dunvorgan," said he, at length,
"but this is the stranche story; and if the two
lads wass not happen to be on the island, it
would hef been a murder, as sure as death.   Poor
thing! that was to hef been marriet this ferry

day. We will hef the sheriff at Styornoway to inquire into this."

"And what does she say, Mr. Livingston?" asked the farmer.

"Well, you see, Dunvorgan, it is not easy in the dark, where there iss no light to write down a word, to understand such a langwich as the French langwich; but if I do not mek a great mistake, the young leddy was stolen away from her friends, and put on board the smack; and little doubt hef I that the master of the smack wass paid to mek away with her—maype in the night-time, if there wass no one seeing. She iss from Morlaix, that iss on the coast of Brittany; and any one that iss well-read, and acquented with geography and other things, knows that the people of Brittany are ferry revencheful people. But the young leddy she wass making a prayer to the master of the smack; and maype he wass afrait; or maype he thought that leaving her on an island wass ass goot ass anything to put her away—ay! ay! the poor young lass that wass to hef been marriet this ferry day mirover!"

"Mr. Livingston, some one will hef to answer for this; what do you think now?"

"That is what I think. And we will get at the story better when we hef the sheriff from Styornoway ; and the sheriff's leddy—oh, she is wonderful goot at ahl langwiches, except the Gaelic, and she is not so goot at the Gaelic : and the sheriff will be for taking the young leddy over to Styornoway, no doubt, and putting her on board of the *Clansman*, and sending her back to her friends. And the goot heart of her ! do you know what she hass been offering to me ? "

"How can I know ? "

" She wass wanting me to tck her gold rings and her gold watch and chain, too ; and to gif them to the boys for their kindness. Do you hear that, now, Colin, and you, too, Archie ? But I would not hef her go away back to France, and be speaking to the French people, and be saying that the Highland people would tek money for a kindness. I would not hef any one say that."

" That iss right, Mr. Livingston ; my boy Colin would tek no money for being of help to any one. And if he would tek money, then it iss a stick I would tek to his back, to gif him a little goot manners. But it iss a stranche thing that the master of the yacht, if he wass such a scoundrel as that, wass not for stealing the young leddy's watch and other things too."

"Dunvorgan," said the schoolmaster, thoughtfully, " I will tell you my opinion now—that the master of the smack wass afrait of what he had done, and wass glad to get her away out of the smack without thinking of anything else. And I suppose he wass thinking that if he left her on Farriskeir, no one would effer see or hear of her again—that she would go mad and drown herself, maype—ay, ay—and ferry likely that would hef happened but for the two young lads —it wass a very stranche chance."

When they reached the shore on the other side it was close on midnight; but all the same there were near a dozen people waiting for them; and great was the wonderment among the folk when they heard the strange news. And they were civil enough not to stare at the young French lady ; but they were very kind to her ; and she was taken up to Dunvorgan farm, where they got some supper for her, and some tea, and gave her a bedroom all to herself— which is a luxury in those parts. And amid all this the lads found occasion to have a little talk between themselves—of course in Gaelic.

"There is one good thing, Archie, that every one is taken up with the young French lady ; and my father has not said anything about the loss of the boat."

"And I do not think they will say anything now, Colin; for three lives are better than a boat."

"But it is hard on my father, Archie, that he should have to pay for another boat."

However, as it turned out, the new boat was paid for in quite an unexpected way. For when the sheriff of Stornoway had learned all this story, and when he had communicated with the young lady's friends in Brittany, there was, of course, a great commotion ; and the two lads had to go over to Stornoway to give evidence there before some gentlemen sent all the way over from France for the purpose.

Then the young lady left with these gentle-men (though ·it seemed as if she would never cease expressing to the two lads, through the sheriff, her gratitude to them), and no one ex-pected to hear any more of the thing, except the sheriff, who knew better.

One day Colin M'Calmont and Archie Living-ston, with their respective fathers, were summoned to go over to Stornoway, to the sheriff's office ; and they went.

"I have got the reward now, for you two boys," said he.

"What reward?" they both said at once.

"The reward that was offered in the French papers for information about that young lady when she was found to be missing."

He showed them an oblong piece of paper.

"It is five thousand francs ; do you know how much that is ?"

"I do not," said Colin ; and the schoolmaster's son looked doubtful.

"I suppose you can divide by twenty-five, surely ?" said he, good-naturedly.

"That would come to two hundred pounds," said the younger lad.

"Very well, then. That piece of paper is worth two hundred pounds; and that is one hundred pounds for each of you. If I were you, I would put it in the savings-bank ; and when you grow up, it would be a fine thing for you."

"I will not do that, sir," said Colin M'Calmont.

"What then ?"

G

"I will buy a boat for my father as good as the one that was sunk—ay, and better, too. And if there is anything over, that is what I will put into the savings-bank."

"But wait a minute, my lad. This five thousand francs is the reward offered by Mademoiselle Desclin's guardians—for she has neither father nor mother; but she wishes to add something to show that she does not forget your kindness to her. She wishes to be allowed to give you a boat, sails and all complete, similar to the one that was sunk; only it is to be your own. But that will do for your father as well as for yourself."

"Surely, surely," said Dunvorgan. "Let the lad have the whole of the hundred pounds put in the bank in his own name. It will be a good thing for him when he will take a farm for himself."

"And you, Archie Livingston; I am to buy you a silver watch. And if I were you I would sit down and write the young lady a letter in very good English. And there is another thing, Colin, my lad; she wants you to have the boat called the *Félicité*—for that is her own name; and you can have no objection to that."

"Surely no, sir; and will I write her a letter, too?"

"You could not do better. And so that is all settled. But wait a minute, my lads; I think the next time you go out to frighten the Frenchmen from stealing the sheep at Farris-keir, you'd better leave the pistol ashore; you might get into trouble. And perhaps if the Government were to send the *Jackal* round that way once or twice about this time of the year, that would give them a greater fright than any horse-pistol."

So that was the end of the adventure; and if you should happen on the west coast of Lewis to run against a smart little cutter called the *Félicité*, and should wonder at the name, they will tell you the story there about the two boys who went to frighten the French fishermen away from Farriskeir and Rua-veg.

THE FOUR MACNICOLS.

THE FOUR MACNICOLS.

CHAPTER I.

JUVENTUS MUNDI.

It was on a bright and glorious morning in July that the great chieftain, Robert of the Red Hand, accompanied by his kinsmen and allies, put to sea in his war-galley, resolved to sweep the Spanish main free of all his enemies, and thereafter to hold high revel in the halls of Eilean-na-Rona. At least, that was how it appeared to the imagination of the great chieftain himself, though the simple facts of the case were a trifle less romantic. For this Robert of the Red Hand, more familiarly known as Rob MacNicol, or even as plain Rob, was an active, stout-sinewed, black-eyed lad of seventeen, whose only mark of chieftainship apparently was that, unlike his brothers, he wore shoes and stockings; these three relatives con-

stituted his allies and kinsmen; the so-called
Spanish main was in reality an arm of the sea
better known in the Hebrides as Loch Scrone;
and the war-galley was an old, ramshackle,
battered, and be-tarred boat belonging generally
to the fishing village of Erisaig; for, indeed, the
boat was so old and so battered that nobody
now seemed to claim any special ownership of it.

These four MacNicols,—Robert, Neil, Nicol,
and Duncan,—were, it must be admitted, an
idle and graceless set, living for the most part a
hand-to-mouth, amphibious, curlew-like kind of
life, and far more given to aimless voyages in
boats not belonging to them than inclined to
turn their hand to any honest labour. But this
must be said in their excuse, that no boy or lad
born in the village of Erisaig could by any
means whatsoever be brought to think of be-
coming anything else than a fisherman. It was
impossible to induce them to apprentice themselves to any ordinary trade. They would wait
until they were old enough to go after the
herring, like the others; that was man's work;
that was something like; that was different from
staying ashore and twiddling one's fingers over a
pair of somebody else's shoes, or laboriously

shaping a block of sandstone for somebody else's
house. This Rob MacNicol, for example: it was
only for want of a greater career that he had
constituted himself a dreaded sea-rover, a stern
chieftain, etc., etc. His secret ambition—his
great and constant and secret ambition—went
far further than that. It was to be of man's
estate, broad-shouldered and heavy-bearded; to
wear huge black boots up to his thighs, and a
blue flannel jersey; to have a peaked cap (not
forgetting a brass button on each side by way of
smartness); and then to come along, in the
afternoon, with a yellow oilskin tied up in a
bundle, to the wharf where the herring fleet lay,
the admiration and the envy of all the miserable
creatures condemned to stay ashore.

In the meantime—in these days of joyous
idleness, while as yet the cares and troubles
which this history will have to chronicle were
far away from him and his simply because they
were unknown—Rob MacNicol, if he could not
be a fisherman, could be an imaginary chieftain,
and in that capacity he gave his orders as one
who knew how to make himself obeyed. As
soon as they had shoved the boat clear of the
smacks, the jib was promptly set; the big lumps

of stone that served for ballast were duly shifted; the lug-sail, as black as pitch and full of holes, was hoisted, and the halyards made fast; then the sheet was hauled in by Nicol MacNicol, who had been ordered to the helm; and finally the shaky old nondescript craft began to creep through the blue waters of Erisaig Bay. It was a lovely morning; the light breeze from the land seemed steady enough; altogether, nothing could have been more auspicious for the setting out of the great chieftain and his kinsmen.

But great as he is, he is not above fearing the criticism of people ashore on his method of handling a boat. Rob, from his proud position at the bow, darted an angry glance at his helmsman.

"Keep her full, will ye?" he growled in an undertone. "Do ye call that steering, ye gomeril? Run her by Daft Sandy's boat! It is no better than a cowherd you are at the steering."

This daft Sandy, who will turn up in our history by and by, was a half-witted old man, who spent his life in fishing for flounders from a rotten old punt he had become possessed of. He earned a sort of living that way; and

seldom went near the shore during the day
except to beg for a herring or two for bait,
when the boats came in. He got the bait, but
in an ignominious way; for the boys, stripping
the nets, generally saved up the "broken"
herring in order to pelt Daft Sandy with the
fragments when he came near. That is to say,
they indulged in this amiable sport except when
Rob MacNicol happened to be about. That
youth had been heard to remark that the first
he caught at this game would pay a sudden visit
to the dead dog-fish lying beneath the clear
waters of the harbour; and it was very well
known among the urchins of Erisaig that the
eldest MacNicol had very little scruple about
taking the law into his own hand. When he
found a bigger boy thrashing a smaller one, he
invariably thrashed the bigger one, just to keep
things even, as it were; and he had invented
for the better guidance of his brethren and
associates a series of somewhat stringent rules
and punishments, to which, it must be acknow-
ledged, he cheerfully submitted himself. At
the same time, he was aware that even the
most moral and high-principled government has
occasionally to assert itself with rude physical

force; and although his hand was not particularly red, as might have been expected, it was uncommonly hard, and a cuff from it was understood to produce the most startling lightning effects in the region of the eye.

Well, as they were nearing Daft Sandy's punt, Rob called out to him,—

"Sandy, have ye had any luck the day?"

The little, bent, blear-eyed old man looked up from his hand-lines.

"No mich."

As the boat was gliding past Rob flung a couple of herring into the punt.

"There's some bait for ye."

"Ay; and where are ye for going, Robert?" the old man said, as they passed. "Tak' heed. It's squally outside."

There was no answer; for at this moment the quick eye of the chieftain detected one of his kinsmen in the commission of a heinous crime. Tempted by the light and steady breeze, Nicol had given way to idleness, and had made fast the main-sheet, instead of holding it in his hand, ready for all emergencies. This, and not unnaturally, on such a squally coast, Rob MacNicol had constituted an altogether unforgivable

offence ; and his first impulse was to jump down
to the stern of the boat and give the helmsman,
caught *in flagrante delicto*, a sounding whack on
the side of the head. But a graver sense of
justice prevailed. He summoned a court-martial.
Nicol, catching the eye of his brother, hastily
tried to undo the sheet from the pin ; but it was
too late. The crime had been committed ; there
were two witnesses, besides the judge, who was
also the jury. The judge and jury forthwith
pronounced sentence : Nicol MacNicol to forfeit
one penny to the fund being secretly stored up
for the purchase of a set of bag-pipes, or to be
lowered by the shoulders until his feet should
touch the ground in the dungeon of Eilean-na-
Rona Castle. He was left to decide which alternative he would accept ; and it must be said
that the culprit, after a minute or two's sulking,
perceived the justice of the sentence, and calmly
said he would take the dungeon.

"Ye think I'm feared ? " he said contemptuously, to Neil and Duncan, who were grinning
at him. " Wha was it that gruppit the whutte-
ruck ? * And is there anything worse than
whutterucks in that hole in the castle ? "

* *Anglicè*, seized hold of the weasel.

"Ye'll find out, Nicol, my man," said his cousin Neil. "There's warlocks. And they'll grup ye by the legs."

"I'll save the penny anyway," said Nicol, to whom a penny was a thing of known and substantial value.

Now if any proof had been needed that Rob MacNicol's stringent sailing rules were a matter of stern necessity, it was quickly forthcoming. On this beautiful summer morning, with the sea smooth and blue around them, they were sailing along as pleasantly as might be. But they had scarcely got through the narrow channel leading from the harbour, and were just emerging into Loch Scrone, when a squall of wind came tearing along and hit the boat so that the lug-sail was almost flattened on to the water.

"Run her up! Haul in your sheet!" yelled Rob to the frightened steersman.

Well it was at such a moment that the main sheet was free to be hauled in; for as the bow was put up to the wind, the varying squall caught her on the other beam and threw her over, so that she shipped a bucket or two of water. Had the water got into the belly of the sail the weight would have dragged her down ; but Rob instantly got rid of this danger by springing to the halyards, and, the moment the crank craft strove to right herself, bringing sail and yard rattling down into the boat. By this time, so fierce was the squall, a pretty heavy sea had sprung up, and altogether things looked very ugly. When they allowed the jib to fill, even that was enough to send the boat over, and she had already a dangerous lot of water surging among the ballast; while, when they were forced to put her head to the wind, she drifted with a heavily running tide, and right to leeward was a long reef of rocks that would inevitably crunch her into matchwood. The younger brothers said not a word, but looked at Rob, ready to obey his slightest gesture, and Rob stood by the mast calling out from time to time to Nicol.

Matters grew worse. It was no use trying merely to keep her head to the wind, for she was drifting rapidly, and the first shock on the rocks would send her and her stone ballast to the bottom. On the other hand, there was no open sea-room to let her run away before the wind with a straining jib. At all hazards it was

necessary to fight her clear of that long ledge of
rock, even if the wind threatened to tear the
mast out of the boat. So Rob himself sprang
down to the stern and took the tiller.

"Duncan, Neil, stand by the halyards now !
When I sing out to ye, hoist her—be ready
now ! "

He had his eye on the rocks all this time.
On the highest of them was a tall iron perch,
painted scarlet—a warning to sailors ; but from
that point long shelves and spurs ran out, the
yellow surface of barnacles growing greener and
greener as they went deeper into the sea. Already Rob MacNicol could make out some of
these submarine reefs even through the turbu-
lent water.

"Now then, boys; up with her ! Quick
now ! "

It was a venturesome business ; but there was
no help for it. The moment the sail was half
hoisted, a gust caught the boat and drove her
over until her gunwale again scooped up a lot of
the hissing water. But as she righted, staggering
all the while, it was clear there was some good
way on her, and Rob, having had recourse to
desperate remedies, was determined to give her

enough of the wind. Down again went the gunwale to the hissing water; and the strain on the rotten sheets of the old boat was so great that it was a wonder everything did not go by the board. But now there was a joyous hissing of foam at the bow; she was forging ahead; if she could only stand the pressure, in a minute or so she would be clear of the rocks. Rob still kept his eye on these treacherous shelves of yellow-green. Then he sang out,—

"Down with her, boys!"

The black lug-sail rattled into the boat; there was nothing left now but the straining jib.

"Slack the lee jib-sheet!"

The next minute he had put his helm gently up; the bow of the boat fell away from the wind; and presently—just as they had time to see the green depths of the rocks they had succeeded in weathering—the war-galley of the great chieftain was spinning away down Loch Scrone, racing with the racing waves, the wind tearing and hauling at her bellied-out jib.

"Hurrah, my lads! we'll soon be at Eilean-na-Rona now, eh?" Rob shouted.

He did not seem much put about by that narrow escape. Squalls were common on this coast, and it was the business of one aspiring to be a fisherman to take things as they came.

"Come, set to work and bale out the boat, you bare-shanks lot! How d'ye think she can sail with the half of Loch Scrone inside her?"

Thus admonished, the younger brothers were soon among the stone ballast baling out the surging water with such rude utensils as they could find. But the squall was of no great duration. The wind moderated in force; then it woke up again, and brought a smart shower of rain across; then, as if by magic, the heavens suddenly cleared, a burst of hot sunlight fell around them, the sea grew intensely blue, the far hills on the other side of Loch Scrone began to shine green in the yellow light, and all that was left to tell of the squall that had very nearly put an end to the great chieftain and all his clan was a quickly-running sea, now all sparkling in diamonds.

The danger being thus over, Rob once more delivered the tiller into the charge of his brother Nicol, and went forward to his post of observation at the bow. About the only bit of the imaginative voyage on which he had started that had a solid basis in fact was the existence

of an old castle—or rather the ruins of what had
once been a castle—on the island called Eilean-
na-Rona ; and now that they were racing down
Loch Scrone, that small island was drawing
nearer, and already they could make out the
dark tower and ivied walls of the ancient keep.
Far darker than the tower itself were the legends
connected with this stronghold of former times ;
but for these the brothers MacNicol, who had
seized on the place as their own, cared little. It
is true, they had some dread of the dungeon,
and none of them would have liked to visit
Eilean-na-Rona at night ; but in the daytime
the old ruins formed an excellent retreat, where
they could play such high jinks or hold such
courtly tournaments as they chose.

They ran the boat into a little creek of the
uninhabited island, driving her right up on the
beach for safety's sake, there being no anchor.
Then—Neil carrying a small basket the while
and Duncan a coil of rope—they passed through
a wood of young larches and spruce, the air
smelling strongly of bracken and meadow-sweet
after the rain ; and finally they reached the
rocky eminence on which stood the ruins. There
was no way up, for tourists did not come that

way, and the owner of the island, who was a
farmer on the mainland, had but little care for
antiquities. However, the lads found no difficulty. They swarmed up the face of the crags
like so many squirrels, and found themselves on
a grassy plateau which had once formed the
outer courtyard of the keep. Around this
plateau were fragments of what in former days
had been a massive wall, but most of the
crumbling masonry was hidden under ivy and
weeds. In front of them, again, rose the great
tower with its arched and gloomy entrance, and
its one or two small windows, in the clefts of
which bunches of wallflower were growing. The
only sign of life about the old castle or the
uninhabited island was given by two or three
jackdaws that wheeled about overhead, and
cawed harshly in resentment of this intrusion.

The great chieftain, Robert of the Red Hand,
having now assembled his kinsmen and allies in
the ancient halls of Eilean-na-Rona, proceeded to
speak as follows :

" Nicol, my man, ye have been tried and convicted."

" I ken that," was Nicol's philosophical reply.

" Ye had no business to make fast the sheet

of the lug-sail; ye might have drooned the lot of us."

Nicol nodded. He had sinned, and was prepared to suffer.

"Have ye aught to say against your being lowered into the dungeon?"

"I have not. Do you think I'm feared?" said Nicol scornfully.

"Ye will not pay the penny?"

"Deil a penny will I pay!"

"Nicol," said his cousin Neil, with some touch of compassion—for indeed he knew that the dungeon was a gruesome place—"Nicol, maybe you have not got a penny?"

"Well, I have not," said Nicol.

"Will I lend ye one?"

"What would be the use of that?" said Nicol; "I would have to pay it back. Do you think I'm feared? I tell you I am not feared."

So there was nothing for it but to get the rope and pass it under Nicol's arms, fastening it securely at his back. Thus bound, the culprit was marched through the archway of the old tower into an apartment that was but feebly lit by the reflected glare coming from without. The other boys, as well as Nicol, walked very carefully over the dank-smelling earth, until they came to what seemed to be a large hole dug out of the ground, and black as midnight. This was the dungeon into which Nicol was to be lowered, that he might expiate his offence before the high revels began.

CHAPTER II.

THE LAST OF THE GAMES.

BUT before proceeding to relate how the captive clansman was lowered into the dungeon of the castle on Eilean-na-Rona, it will be necessary to explain why he did not choose to purchase his liberty by the payment of the sum of one penny. Pennies among the boys of Erisaig, and more especially among the MacNicols, were an exceedingly scarce commodity. The father of the three MacNicols, who was also burdened with the charge of their orphan cousin Neil, was a hand on board the steamer *Glenara Castle*, and very seldom came ashore. He had but small wages; and it was all he could do, in the bringing up of the boys, to pay a certain sum for their lodging and schooling, leaving them pretty much to cadge for themselves as regarded food and clothes. Their food, mostly porridge, potatoes, and fish of their own catching, cost

little ; and they did not spend much money on
clothes, especially in summer time, when no
Erisaig boy—except Rob MacNicol, who was a
distinguished person—would submit to the en-
cumbrance of shoes and stockings. Nevertheless,
for various purposes, money was necessary to
them ; and this they obtained by going down
in the morning, when the herring boats came in,
and helping the men to strip the nets. The
men were generally tired out and sleepy with
their long night's work ; and if they had had
anything like a good haul, they were glad to
give these lads twopence or threepence apiece to
undertake the labour of lifting the nets, yard by
yard, out of the hold, shaking out the silvery
fish and dexterously extricating those that had
got more firmly enmeshed. Moreover, it was a
work the boys delighted in. If it was not the
rose, it was near the rose. If it was not for
them as yet to sail away in the afternoon,
watched by all the village, at least they could
take this small part in the great herring trade.
And when they had shaken out the last of the
nets, and received their wages, they stepped
ashore with a certain pride ; and generally they
put both hands in their pockets as a real fisher-

man would do ; and perhaps they would walk along the quays with a slight lurch, as if they, also, had been cramped up all the long night through, and felt somewhat unused to walking on first getting back to land.

Now these MacNicol boys, again imitating the well-to-do among the fishermen, had each an account at the savings bank ; and the pence they got were carefully hoarded up. For if they wanted a new Glengarry cap, or if they wanted to buy a book telling them of all kinds of tremendous adventures at sea, or if it became necessary to purchase some more fishing-hooks at the grocer's shop, it was their own small store of wealth they had to look to ;. and so it came about that a penny was something to be seriously considered. When Rob MacNicol had to impose a fine of one penny, he knew it was a dire punishment; and if there was any alternative the fine was rarely paid. The fund, therefore, which he had started for the purchase of an old and disused set of bagpipes, and which was to be made up of those fines, did not grow apace. Of course, being a chieftain, he must needs have a piper. The revels in the halls of Eilean-na-Rona lacked half their impressiveness

through the want of the pipes. No doubt Rob
had a sort of suspicion that, if ever they should
grow rich enough to buy the old set of bagpipes,
he would have to play them himself; but even
the most ignorant person can perceive that to
be one's own piper must at least be better than
to have no piper at all.

And now the captive Nicol MacNicol was led
to the edge of this black pit in the floor of the
lower hall of the castle. On several occasions
one or other of the boys had been lowered, for
slighter offences, into this dungeon; but no one
had ever been condemned to go to the bottom
—if bottom there were. But Nicol did not
flinch. He was satisfied of the justice of his
sentence. He was aware he deserved the
punishment. Above all, he was determined to
save that penny.

At the same time, when the other three had
poised themselves so as to lower the rope
gradually, and when he found himself descending
into that black hole, he looked rather nervously
below him. Of course he could see nothing.
But there was a vague tradition that this
dungeon was haunted by ghosts, vampires, warlocks, and other unholy things; and there was a

chill, strange, earthy odour arising from it; and the walls that he scraped against were slimy and damp. He uttered no word, however; and those above kept slowly paying out the coil of rope.

Rob became somewhat concerned.

" It'll be no easy job to pull him back," he said in a whisper.

" It's as deep as the dungeon they put Donald Gorm Môr into," said his cousin Neil.

" Maybe there's no bottom at all," said Duncan, rather awe-stricken.

Suddenly a fearful thing happened. There was a cry from below—a quick cry of alarm; and at the same moment they were startled by a wild whizzing and whirring around them, as if a legion of fiends had rushed out of the pit. With a shriek of fright Duncan sprang back from the edge of the dungeon; and that with such force that he knocked over his two companions. Moreover, in falling, they let go the rope; when they rose again they looked round in the twilight, but could find no trace of it. It had slipped over the edge. And there was no sound from below.

Rob was the first to regain his senses. He rushed to the edge of the hole and stooped over.

" Nicol, are ye there ? "

His heart jumped within him when he heard his brother's voice.

" Yes, I am ; and the rope too.   How am I to get up ? "

Rob turned quickly.

" Duncan, down to the boat with ye ! Loosen the lug-sail halyards, and bring them up—quick, quick ! "

Duncan was off like a young roe. He slid down the crags ; he dashed through the larch-wood ; he jumped into the boat on the beach. Presently he was making his way as quickly back again, the halyards coiled round his arm so as not to prevent his climbing.

" Nicol ! " shouted Rob.

" Ay ? "

" I am lowering the halyards to ye.   Fasten them to the end of the rope."

" I canna see them."

" Grope all round till ye come to them."

And so, in process of time, the end of the rope was hauled up, and thereafter—to the great relief of every one—and to his own, no doubt, Nicol appeared alive and well, though somewhat anxious to get away from the neighbourhood of that dungeon. He went immediately out into the warm summer air, followed by the others.

"Man, what a fright I got!" he said at last, having recovered his speech.

"Ay, and so did we," Neil admitted.

"What was't?" said he, timidly; as if almost afraid to put his own fears and suspicions into words.

"I dinna ken," Neil said, looking rather frightened.

"Ye dinna ken!" Rob MacNicol said, with a scornful laugh. "Ye ought to ken, then. It was nothing but a lot of bats; and Duncan yelled as if he had seen twenty warlocks; and knocked us over, so that we lost the rope. Come! boys, begin your games now; the steamer will be in early the day."

Well, it seemed easier to dismiss superstitious fears out here in the sunlight. Perhaps it had been only bats after all. Warlocks did not whirr in the air—at least, they were understood not to do so. Witches were supposed to reserve their aerial performances for the night-time. Perhaps it was only bats, as Rob asserted. Indeed, it would be safer—especially in Rob's presence—to accept his explanation of the mystery. At the same time the younger boys occasionally darted a stealthy glance backward to that gloomy apartment that had so suddenly become alive with unknown things.

Then the games began. Rob had come to the conclusion that a wise chieftain should foster a love for national sports and pastimes; and to that end he had invented a system of marks, the winning of a large number of which entitled the holder to pecuniary or other reward. As for himself, his part was that of spectator and arbiter; he handicapped the competitors; he declared the prizes. On this occasion he ensconced himself in a niche of the ruins, where he was out of the glare of the sun and gracefully surrounded by masses of ivy; while his relatives hauled out to the middle of the green plateau several trunks of fir-trees, of various sizes, that had been carefully lopped and pruned for the purpose of "tossing the caber." Well, they "tossed the caber," they "put the stone," they had wrestling-matches and other trials of strength, Rob the while surveying the scene with a critical eye, and reckoning up the proper number of marks. But now some milder diversions followed. Three or four planks, rudely nailed together, and forming a piece of rough flooring about two or three yards square, were hauled out from an archway, placed on the grass, and a piece of tarpaulin thrown over it. Then two of the boys took out their Jew's-harps—alas! alas! that was the only musical instrument within their reach, until the coveted bagpipes should be purchased—and gaily struck up with "Green grow the rashes, O!" as a preliminary flourish. What was this now? What but a performance of the famous sword-dance by that renowned and valiant henchman, Nicol MacNicol of Erisaig, in the kingdom of Scotland! Nicol, failing a couple of broad-swords or four dirks, had got two pieces of rusty old iron and placed them cross-wise on the extemporised floor. With what skill and nimbleness he proceeded to execute this sword-dance,—which is no doubt the survival of some ancient mystic rite,—with what elegance he pointed his toes and held his arms akimbo; with what amazing dexterity, in all the evolu-tions of the dance, he avoided touching the bits of iron; nay, with what intrepidity, at the most critical moment, he held his arms aloft and

victoriously snapped his thumbs, it wants a
Homeric chronicler to tell. It needs only be
said here that, after it, Neil's "Highland Fling"
was a comparative failure, though he, better
than most, could give that outflung quiver of
the foot which few can properly acquire, and
without which the dancer of the "Highland
Fling" might just as well go home and go to
bed. The great chieftain, having regarded these
and other performances with an observant eye,
and having awarded so many marks to this
one and to that, declared the games over, and
invited the competitors one and all to a royal
banquet.

It was a good deal more wholesome than most
banquets, for it consisted of a scone and a glass
of fresh milk apiece—butter being as yet beyond
the means of the MacNicols. And it was a
good deal more sensible than most banquets, for
there was no speech-making after it. But there
was some interesting conversation.

"Nicol, what did ye find in the dungeon?"
Duncan said.

"Oh, man, it was a gruesome place," said
Nicol, who did not want to make too little of
the perils he had encountered.

"What did ye see?"

"How could I see anything? But I felt plenty on the way down; and I'm sure it's fu' o' creeping things and beasts. And then when I was near the foot, I put my hand on something leevin', and it flew up and hit me; and in a meenit the whole place was alive. Man, what a noise it was! And then down came the rope, and I fell; and I got sich a clour on the head!"

"Nothing but bats!" said Rob, contemptuously.

"I think it was houlets,"* said Duncan, confidently; "for there was one in the wood when I was gaun through, and I nearly ran my head against him. He was sitting in one of the larches—man, he made a noise!"

"Ye've got your heads filled with nothing but witches and warlocks the day!" said Rob, impatiently, as he rose to his feet. "Come, and get the things into the basket. We maun be back in Erisaig before the *Glenara* comes in."

Very soon thereafter the small party made their way down again to the shore, and entered the war-galley of the chieftain, the halyards being restored to their proper use. There were

* *Anglicè,* owls.

no more signs of any squall; but the light steady breeze was contrary; and as Robert of the Red Hand was rather anxious to get back before the steamer should arrive, and as he prided himself on his steering, he himself took the tiller, his cousin Neil being posted as look-out forward.

It was a tedious business this beating up against the contrary wind; but there was nothing the MacNicols delighted in so much as in sailing, and they had grown to be expert in handling a boat. And it needed all their skill to get anything out of these repeated tacks with this old craft, that had a sneaking sort of fashion of falling away to leeward. However, they had the constant excitement of putting about; and the day was fine; and they were greatly refreshed after their arduous pastimes by that banquet of scones and milk. Nor did they know that this was to be the last day of their careless boyish idleness; that never again would the great chieftain, heedless of what the morrow might bring forth, hold these high frolics in the halls of Eilean-na-Rona.

Patience and perseverance will beat even contrary winds; and at last, after one long tack stretching almost to the other side of Loch

Scrone, they put about and managed to make the entrance to the harbour, just weathering the rocks that had nearly destroyed them on their setting out. But here another difficulty waited them. Under the shelter of the low-lying hills, the harbour was in a dead calm. No sooner had they passed the rocks than they found themselves on water as smooth as glass, and there were no oars in the boat. For this oversight Rob MacNicol was not responsible ; the fact being that oars were valuable in Erisaig, and not easily to be borrowed, whereas this old boat was at anybody's disposal. There was nothing for it but to sit and wait for a puff of wind.

Suddenly they heard a sound—the distant throbbing of the *Glenara's* paddles. Rob grew anxious. This old boat was right in the fairway of the steamer ; and the question was whether, in coming round the point, she would see them in time to slow.

" I wish we were out of here," said he.

As a last resource, he threw the tiller into the boat, took up the helm, and tried to use this as a sort of paddle. But this was scarcely of any avail; and they could hear, though they could not see, that the steamer was almost at the point.

The next moment she appeared; and it seemed to them in their fright that she was almost upon them—towering away over them with her gigantic bulk. They heard the scream of the steam-whistle, and the sharp "ping! ping!" of the indicator, as the captain tried to have the engines reversed.

It was too late. The way on the steamer carried her on, even when her paddles were stopped; and the next second her bows had gone clean into the old tarred boat, cutting her almost in two and heeling her over.

She sank at once. Then the passengers of the steamer rushed to the side to see what should become of the lads struggling in the water; the mate threw overboard to them a couple of life-buoys; and the captain shouted out to have a boat lowered. There was a great confusion.

Meanwhile, all this had been witnessed by the father of the MacNicols, who had stood for a second or two as if paralysed. Then a sort of spasm of action seized him, and, apparently not knowing what he was about, he threw open the gangway abaft the paddle-box and sprang into the sea.

CHAPTER III.

ALTERED CIRCUMSTANCES.

EVEN with this big steamer coming right down on them, Rob MacNicol did not lose his head. He knew that his two brothers and his cousin Neil could swim like water-rats; and as for himself, though he would have given a good deal to get rid of his boots, he did not fear being able to get ashore.

But there was no time to think.

"Jump clear of the boat!" he shouted to his companions.

The next second came the dreadful crash. The frail old boat seemed to be pressed onwards and downwards, as if the steamer had run right over her. Then Rob found himself in the water, and very deep in the water too. The next thing he perceived was a great greenish-white thing over his head; and as he knew that that was the hull of the steamer, he struck away from it with all the strength at his disposal. He remembered afterwards experiencing a sort of hatred of that shining green thing, and thinking it looked hideous and dangerous, like a shark.

However, the next moment he rose to the surface, blew the water out of his mouth, and looked around. There was a life-buoy within a yard of him, and the people on the steamer were calling to him to lay hold of it; but he had never touched one of these things, and he preferred to trust to himself, heavy as he felt his boots to be. It was the others he was looking after. Neil, he perceived, was already off for the shore, swimming hand over hand, as if a sword-fish were after him. Nicol was being hauled up the side of the steamer at the end of a rope, just as he had been hauled up from the Eilean-na-Rona dungeon; and his brother Duncan had seized hold of the helm that had been cast loose when the boat went down. Satisfied that every one was safe, Rob himself struck out for the side of the steamer, and was speedily hauled on board, presently finding himself on deck with his two dripping companions.

The strange thing was that his father was nowhere to be seen, and even the captain looked round and asked where John MacNicol was. At the same moment a woman, all trembling, came forward and asked the mate if they had got the man out.

"What man?" said he.

She said she had been standing by the paddle-box, and that one of the sailors, the moment the accident had occurred, had opened the gangway and jumped into the water, no doubt with the intention of rescuing the boys. She had not seen him come up again, for just as he went down the steamer backed.

At this news there was some little consternation. The mate called aloud for John MacNicol; there was no answer. He ran to the other side of the steamer; nothing was visible on the smooth water. They searched everywhere, and the boat that had been lowered was pulled about, but the search was in vain. The woman's story was the only explanation of this strange disappearance; but the sailors suspected more than they dared to suggest to the bewildered lads. They suspected that old Mac-Nicol had dropped into the water just before the paddles had made their first backward revolution, and that in coming to the surface he had been struck by one of the floats. They said nothing of this, however; and as the search proved to be quite useless, the *Glenara* steamed slowly onward to the quay.

It was not until the next afternoon that they recovered the body of old MacNicol; and from certain appearances on the corpse, it was clear that he had been struck down by the paddles in his effort to reach and help his sons. That was a sad evening for Rob MacNicol. It was his first introduction to the cruel facts of life. And amid his sorrow for the loss of one who, in a sort of rough and reticent way, had been very kind and even affectionate to him, Rob was vaguely aware that on himself now rested the responsibility for the upbringing of his two brothers and his cousin. He sat up late that night, long after the others were asleep, thinking of what he should do. In the midst of this silence the door was quietly opened, and Daft Sandy came into the small room.

"What do ye want at this time o' night?" said Rob angrily, for he had been startled.

The old, bent, half-witted man looked

cautiously at the bed, in which Neil lay fast asleep.

"Whisht, Rob, my man," he said in a whisper; "I waited till every one in Erisaig was asleep. Ay, ay! it's a bad day this day for you. And what are ye going to do now, Rob? Ye'll be taking to the fishing?"

"Oh, ay; I'll be taking to the fishing!" said Rob bitterly, for he had been having his dreams also, and had turned from them with a sigh. "Of course I'll be taking to the fishing! And maybe ye'll tell me where I am to get £40 to buy a boat, and where I am to get £30 to buy nets? Maybe ye'll tell me that, Sandy?"

"The bank——"

"What does the bank ken about me? They would as soon think of throwing the money into Loch Scrone."

"But ye ken, Rob, Coll Macdougall would give ye a share in his boat for £12."

"Twelve pounds! Man, ye're just daft, Sandy. Where am I to get £12?"

"Well, well, Rob," said the old man coming nearer, and speaking still more mysteriously, "listen to what I tell ye. Some day or other ye'll be taking to the fishing; and when that

day comes I will put something in your way.
Ay, ay; the fishermen about Erisaig dinna know
everything; come to me, Rob, my man, and I'll
tell ye something about the herring. Ye are a
good lad, Rob; many's the herring I've got from
ye when I wouldna go near the shore for they
mischievous bairns; and when once ye have a
boat and nets o' your own I will tell ye something. Daft Sandy is no so daft, maybe. Have
ye ony tobacco, Rob?"

Rob said he had no tobacco; and making sure
that Daft Sandy had come to him with a pack
of nonsense merely as an excuse to borrow
money for tobacco, he bundled him out of the
house and went to bed.

Rob was anxious that his brothers and cousin,
and himself, should present a respectable appear- .
ance at the funeral; and in these humble pre-
parations nearly all their small savings were
swallowed up. The funeral expenses were paid
by the Steamboat Company. Then after the
funeral, the few people who were present de-
parted to their own homes, no doubt imagining
that the MacNicol boys would be able to live as
hitherto they had lived—that is, anyhow.

But there was a kindly man called Jamieson,

who kept the grocery shop, and he called Rob in
as the boys passed home.

"Rob," said he, "ye maun be doing something now. There's a cousin of mine has a
whiskey shop in the Saltmarket in Glasgow, and
I could get ye a place there."

Rob's very gorge rose at the notion of his
having to serve in a whiskey shop in Glasgow.
That would be to abandon all the proud
ambitions of his life. Nevertheless, he had
been thinking seriously about the duty he owed
to these lads, his companions, who were now
dependent on him. So he swallowed his pride
and said,—

"How much would he give me?"

"I think I could get him to give ye four
shillings a week. That would keep ye very
well."

"Keep me?" said Rob. "Ay, but what's to
become o' Duncan and Neil and Nicol?"

"They must shift for themselves," the grocer
answered.

"That winna do," said Rob, and he left the
shop.

He overtook his companions and asked them
to go along to some rocks overlooking the har-

bour. They sat down there—the harbour below them with all its picturesque boats, and masses of drying nets, and what not.

" Neil," said Rob to his cousin, " we'll have to think about things now. There will be no more Eilean-na-Rona for us. We have just about as much left as will pay the lodgings this week, and Nicol must go three nights a week to the night school. What we get for stripping the nets 'll no do now."

" It will not," said Neil.

" Mr. Jamieson was offering me a place in Glasgow, but it is not very good, and I think we will do better if we keep together. Neil," said he, " if we had only a net, do ye not think we could trawl for cuddies ? " *

And again he said, " Neil, do ye not think we could make a net for ourselves out of the old rags lying at the shed ? "

And again he said, " Do ye think that Peter, the tailor, would lend us his old boat for a shilling a week ? "

It was clear that Rob had been carefully

---

* "Cuddies" is the familiar name in those parts for young saithe. "Trawling," again, means there the use of an ordinary seine.

considering the details of this scheme of co-
operation. And it was eagerly welcomed, not
only by Neil, but also by the brothers Duncan
and Nicol, who had been frightened by the
thought of Rob going away to Glasgow. The
youngest of all, Nicol, boldly declared that he
could mend nets as well as any man in Erisaig.

No sooner was the scheme thoroughly dis-
cussed, than it was determined, under Rob's
direction, to set to work at once. The woman
who kept the lodgings and cooked their food for
them had intimated to them that they need be
in no hurry to pay her for a week or two until
they should find some employment; but they
had need of money, or the equivalent of money,
in other directions. Might not old Peter, who
was a grumbling and ill-tempered person, insist
on being paid in advance? Then, before they
could begin to make a net out of the torn and
rejected pieces lying about the shed, they must
needs have a ball of twine. So Rob bade his
brothers and cousin go away and get their rude
fishing-rods and betake themselves to the rocks
at the mouth of the harbour, and see what fish
they could get for him during the afternoon.

Meanwhile he himself went along to the shed

which was used as a sort of storage-house by some of the fishermen ; and here he found lying about plenty of pieces of net that had been cast aside in the process of mending. This business of mending the nets is the last straw on the back of the tired-out fisherman. When he has met with an accident to his nets during the night, when he has fouled on some rocks in dragging them in, for example, it is a desperately fatiguing affair to set to work to mend them when he gets ashore, dead beat with the labours of the morning. The fishermen, for what reason I do not know, will not entrust this work to their wives ; they will rather, after having been out all night, keep at it themselves, though they drop off to sleep every few minutes. It is not to be wondered at, then, that often, instead of trying to laboriously mend holes here or there, they should cut out a large piece of torn net bodily and tack on a fresh piece. The consequence is, that in a place like Erisaig there is generally plenty of netting to be got for the asking, which is a good thing for gardeners who want to protect currant bushes from the black-birds, and who will take the trouble to patch the pieces together.

Rob was allowed to pick out a large number of pieces that he thought might serve his purpose ; and these he carried off home. But then came the question of floats and sinkers. Sufficient pieces of cork to form the floats might in time be got about the beach ; but the sinkers had all been removed from the cast-away netting. In this extremity, Rob bethought of rigging up a couple of guy-poles, as the salmon-fishers call them, one for each end of the small seine he had in view ; so that these guy-poles, with a lump of lead at the lower end, would keep the net vertical while it was being dragged through the water. All this took up the best part of the afternoon ; for he had to cadge about before he could get a couple of stout poles ; and he had to bargain with the blacksmith for a lump of lead. Then he walked along to the point where the other MacNicols were busy fishing.

They had been lucky with their lines and bait. On the rocks beside them lay two or three small codling, a large flounder, two good-sized lythe, and nearly a dozen saithe. Rob got hold of these ; washed them clean to make them look fresh and smart; put a string through their gills, and marched off with them to the village.

He felt no shame in trying to sell fish : was it not the whole trade of the village ? He walked into the grocer's shop.

"Will ye buy some fish ?" said he, "they're fresh."

The grocer looked at them.

"What do you want ?"

"A ball of twine."

"Let me tell ye this, Rob," said the grocer, severely, "that a lad in your place should be thinking of something else than fleein' a dragon."*

"I dinna want to flee any dragon," said Rob, "I want to mend a net."

"Oh, that is quite different," said the grocer; and then he added, with a good-natured laugh, "Are ye going to be a fisherman, Rob ?"

"I will see," Rob said.

So he had his ball of twine—and a very large one it was. Off he set to his companions.

"Come away, boys, I have other work for ye. Now, Nicol, my man, ye'll show us what ye can do in the mending of nets. Ye havena been telling lies ?"

Well, it took them several days of very hard

* "Fleein' a dragon"—flying a kite.

and constant work before they rigged up something resembling a small seine; and then Rob affixed his guy-poles; and they went to the grocer and got from him a lot of old rope on the promise to give him a few fresh fish whenever they happened to have a good haul. Then Rob proceeded to his fateful interview with Peter the tailor.

Peter was a sour-visaged, gray-headed old man, who wore horn-rimmed spectacles. He was sitting cross-legged on his bench when Rob entered.

"Peter, will ye lend me your boat?"

"I will not."

"Why will ye no lend me the boat?"

"Do I want it sunk, as ye sunk that boat the other day? Go away with ye. Ye're an idle lot, you MacNicols. Ye'll be drooned some day."

"We want it for the fishing, Peter," said Rob, who took no notice of the tailor's ill-temper. "I'll give ye a shilling a week for the loan o't."

"A shilling a week!" said Peter with a laugh. "A shilling a week! Where's your shilling?"

"There," said Rob, putting it plump down on the bench.

K

The tailor looked at the shilling ; took it up, bit it, and put it in his pocket.

"Very well," said he, "but mind, if ye sink my boat, ye'll have three pounds to pay."

Rob went back eager and joyous. Forthwith, a thorough inspection of the boat was set about by the lads in conjunction ; they tested the oars ; they tested the thole-pins ; they had a new piece of cork put into the bottom. For that evening, when it grew a little more towards dusk, they would make their first cast with their net.

Yes ; and that evening, when it had quite turned to dusk, the people of Erisaig were startled with a new proclamation. It was Neil MacNicol, standing in front of the cottages, and boldly calling forth these words :

"Is there any one wanting Cuddies? There are Cuddies to be sold at the West Slip for a Sixpence a Hundred !"

CHAPTER IV.

FURTHER ENDEAVOUR.

THAT was indeed an anxious time when the four
MacNicols proceeded to try the net on which
they had spent so much forethought and labour.
They had no great expectation of catching fish
this evening; their object was rather to try
whether the ropes would hold, whether the floats
would be sufficient, and whether Rob's guy-poles
would keep the net vertical. So they got into
the tailor's boat, and rowed away round the
point to a sandy bay where they had nothing
to fear from rocks on this their first experiment.

It was, as has been mentioned in the previous
chapter, nearly dusk—an excellent time for
catching saithe, if saithe were about. The net
had been carefully placed in the stern of the
boat, so that it would run out easily, the rope
attached to the guy-pole neatly coiled on the
top. Rob was very silent as his two brothers

pulled away at the long oars. He knew what
depended on this trial. They had just enough
money left to settle with their landlady on the
following evening ; and Nicol's school-fees had
to be paid in advance.

They rowed quietly into this little bay, which,
though of a sandy bottom, was pretty deep.
Rob had resolved to take the whole responsibility of the experiment on himself. He landed
his brothers and his cousin, giving the latter the
end of the rope attached to the guy-pole ; then
he quietly pulled away again from the shore.

When the length of the rope was exhausted,
he himself took the guy-pole and gently dropped
it over, to prevent splashing ; and as he did so
the net began to pay out. He pulled slowly,
just to see how the thing would work; and it
seemed to work very well. The net went out
freely, and apparently sank properly ; from the
top of the guy-pole to the stern of the boat you
could see nothing but the line of the floats on
the smooth water. But the net was a small
one : soon it would be exhausted ; so Rob began
to pull round towards the shore again. At the
same time Neil, who had had his instructions,
began to haul in his end of the net gently, so

that by-and-by, when Rob had run the boat on the beach, and jumped out with his rope in his hand, the line of floats began to form a semi-circle that was gradually narrowing and coming nearer the shore.

It was a moment of great excitement, and not a word was spoken. For although this was ostensibly only a trial to see how the net would work, each lad in his secret heart was wondering whether there might not be a haul of fish captured from the mysterious deep ; and not one of them, not Rob himself, could tell whether this very considerable weight they were gradually pulling in was the weight of the net merely, or the weight of fish, or the weight of sea-weed.

The semicircle of the floats came nearer and nearer, all eyes striving to pierce the clear water.

" I hope the rope'll no break," said Rob, anxiously, for the weight was great.

" And it's only sea-weed ! " said Duncan, in a tone of great disappointment.

But Rob's eye had been caught by some unusual appearance in the water. It seemed troubled somehow ; and more especially near the line of floats.

" Is it ? " said he ; and he hastily bade Duncan take the rope and haul it gently in. He himself began to take up handfuls of small stones, and fling them into the sea close by the two guy-poles, so that the fish should be frightened back into the net. And as the semicircle grew still smaller, it was very obvious that, though there might be sea-weed in the net, it was not all sea-weed. By this time the guy-poles had been got ashore ; they were now hauling at the net itself.

" Quicker now, boys ! " Rob called out. " Man alive, look at that ! "

All the space of water now enclosed by the net was seen to be in a state of commotion ; the net itself was being violently shaken ; here and there a fish leapt into the air.

" Steady, boys ! Don't jerk, or ye'll tear the net to bits ! " Rob called out in great excitement.

For behold ! when they had hauled this great weight up on the shore with a final swoop, there was something there that almost bewildered them—a living mass of fish floundering about in the wet sea-weed—some springing into the air—others flopping out on to the sand—many help-lessly entangled in the meshes. It was a won-

derful sight; but their astonishment and delight
had to give place to action.

"Run for the boat, Nicol! There's more
where they came from!" Rob shouted.

Nicol rushed along to the boat; shoved her
out; pulled her along to where his companions
were; and backed her, stern in. They had no
bucket; they had to fling the fish into the
bottom of the boat. But this business of stripping the nets—shaking out the sea-weed and
freeing the enmeshed fish—was familiar to
them; and they all worked with a will. There
was neither a dog-fish nor a conger in all the
haul, so they had no fears for their hands. In
less than a quarter of an hour the net was back
in the boat, properly arranged, and Rob ready to
start again—at a place farther along the beach.

They were soon full of eagerness. In fact,
they were too eager; and this time they hauled
in with such might and main that, just as the
guy-poles were nearing the shore, the rope
attached to one of them broke. But Rob instantly jumped into the water, seized the pole
itself, and hauled it out with him. Here, also,
they had a considerable take of fish; but there
was a heavy weight of sea-weed besides; and

one or two rents showed that they had pulled
the net over rocks. So they went back to
their former ground; and so successful were
they, and so eagerly did they work, that when
the coming darkness warned them to return to
Erisaig, they had the stern of the boat nearly
full of very fairly-sized saithe.

Neil regarded this wonderful treasure of the
deep as he laboured away at his oar.

"Man, Rob, who could have expected such a
lot? And what will ye do with them now?
Will ye send them to Glasgow by the *Glenara*?
—I think Mr. M'Aulay would lend us a box or
two. Or will ye clean them and dry them, and
sell them from a barrow?"

"We canna start two or three trades all at
once," said Rob, after a minute or two. "I
think we'll sell them straight off, if the folk are
no in bed. Ye'll gang and see, Neil; and I'll
count the fish at the slip."

"And what will I say ye will take for them?"

"I think I would ask a sixpence a hundred,"
said Rob, slowly; for he had been considering
that question for the last ten minutes.

At length they got into the slip; and Neil at
once proceeded to inform the inhabitants of

Erisaig, who were still lounging about in the dusk, that for sixpence a hundred they could have fine fresh "cuddies." It might be thought that in a place like Erisaig, which was one of the headquarters of the herring-trade, it would be difficult to sell fish of any description. But the fact was that the herring were generally contracted for by the agents of the salesmen, and shipped directly for Glasgow, so that they were but rarely retailed in Erisaig itself; moreover, people accustomed to herring their whole life through preferred variety—a freshly-caught mackerel, or flounder, or what not. Perhaps, however, it was more curiosity than anything else that brought the neighbours along to the west slip, to see what the MacNicols had been about.

Well, there was a good deal of laughing and jeering, especially on the part of the men (these were idlers : the fishermen were all gone away in the boats); but the women, who had to provide for their households, knew when they had a cheap bargain ; and the sale of the "cuddies" proceeded briskly. Indeed, when the people had gone away again, and the four lads were by themselves on the quay, there was not a single

" cuddy " left—except a dozen that Rob had put into a can of water, to be given to the grocer in the morning as part payment for the loan of the ropes.

" What do you make it altogether ? " said Neil to Rob, who was counting the money.

" Three shillings and ninepence."

" Three shillings and ninepence ! Man, that's a lot. Will ye put it in the savings bank ? "

" No, I will not," said Rob. " I'm no satisfied with the net, Neil. We must have better ropes all the way round ; and whatever money we can spare we maun spend on the net. Man, think of this now : if we were to fall in with a big haul of herring or Johnnie-Dories, and lose them through the breaking of the net, I think ye would jist sit down and greet."

It was wise counsel, as events showed. For one afternoon, some ten days afterwards, they set out as usual. They had been having varying success ; but they had earned more than enough to pay their landlady, the tailor, and the school-master ; and every farthing beyond these neces-sary expenses they had spent on the net. They had replaced all the rotten pieces with sound twine ; they had got new ropes ; they had

deepened it, moreover, and added some more
sinkers to help the guy-poles. Well, on this
afternoon, Duncan and Nicol, being the two
youngest, were as usual pulling away to one of
the small quiet bays, and Rob was idly looking
around him, when he saw something on the surface of the sea at some distance off that excited
a sudden interest. It was what the fishermen
call " broken water "—a seething produced by a
shoal of fish.

" Look, look, Neil ! " he cried. " It's either
mackerel or herring ; will we try for them ? "

The greatest excitement at once prevailed on
board. The younger brothers pulled their
hardest to make for that rough patch on the
water. Rob undid the rope from the guy-pole,
and got this last ready to drop overboard. He
knew very well that they ought to have had two
boats to execute this manœuvre ; but was there
not a chance for them if they were to row hard,
in a circle, and pick up the other end of the net
when they came to it ? So Neil took a third
oar : two rowing one side and one the other was
just what they wanted.

They came nearer and nearer that strange
hissing of the water. They kept rather away

from it : and Rob quietly dropped the guy-pole over, paying out the net rapidly, so that it should not be dragged after the boat. Then the three lads pulled hard, and in a circle, so that at last they were sending the bow of the boat straight towards the floating guy-pole. The other guy-pole was near the stern of the boat, the rope made fast to one of the thwarts. In a few minutes Rob had caught this first guy-pole : they were now possessed of the two ends of the net.

But the water had grown suddenly quiet. Had the fish dived and escaped them ? There was not the motion of a fin anywhere : and yet the net seemed heavy to haul.

" Rob," said Neil, almost in a whisper, " we've got them ! "

" We havena got them," was the reply ; " but they're in the net. Man, I wonder if it'll stand out."

Then it was that the diligent patching and the strong tackle told. The question was not with regard to the strength of the net, it was rather with regard to the strength of the younger lads ; for they had succeeded in enclosing a goodly portion of a large shoal of mackerel, and the weight seemed more than they could get into the boat. But even the strength of the younger ones seemed to grow into the strength of giants when they saw through the clear water a great moving mass like quicksilver. And then the wild excitement of hauling in ; the difficulty of it ; the danger of the fish escaping ; the warning cries of Rob ; the clatter made by the mackerel ; the possibility of swamping the boat altogether, as all the four were straining their utmost at one side. Indeed, by an awkward tilt at one moment some hundred or two of the mackerel were seen to glide away ; but perhaps that rendered it all the more practicable to get into the boat what remained. When that heaving, sparkling, jerking mass of quicksilver at last was captured —shining all through the brown meshes of the net—the younger lads sat down quite exhausted, wet through, and happy.

" Man, Rob, what do you think of that ? " said Neil in amazement.

" What do I think ? " said Rob ; " I think that if we could get two or three more hauls like that I would soon buy a share in Coll Mac-Dougall's boat and go after the herring."

They had no more thought that afternoon of "cuddy"-fishing after this famous take. Rob and Neil—the younger ones having had their share—rowed back to Erisaig; then Rob left the boat at the slip, and walked up to the office of the fish-salesman.

"What will ye give me for mackerel?" he said.

The salesman laughed at him, thinking he had caught a few with rods and flies.

"I'm no buying mackerel," said he; "no by the half-dozen."

"I've half a boat load," said Rob.

The salesman glanced towards the slip, and saw the tailor's boat pretty low in the water.

"Is that mackerel?"

"Yes, it is mackerel."

"Where were you buying them?"

"I was not buying them anywhere. I caught them myself—my brothers and me."

"I do not believe you."

"I cannot help that, then," said Rob. "But where had I the money to buy mackerel from any one?"

The salesman glanced at the boat again.

"I'll go down to the slip with you."

So he and Rob together walked down to the slip, and the salesman had a look at the mackerel. Apparently he had arrived at the conclusion that, after all, Rob was not likely to have bought a cargo of mackerel as a commercial speculation.

" Well, I will buy the mackerel from you," he said. " I will give you half-a-crown the hundred for them."

" Half-a-crown !" said Rob. " I will take three-and-sixpence the hundred for them."

" I will not give it to you. But I will give you three shillings the hundred, and a good price, too."

" Very well, then," said Rob.

So the MacNicols got altogether £2 : 8s. for that load of mackerel : and out of that Rob spent the eight shillings on still further improving the net; the £2 going into the savings bank. It is to be imagined that after this they kept a pretty sharp look-out for " broken water ; " but of course they could not expect to run across a shoal of mackerel every day.

However, as time went on, with bad luck and with good, and by dint of hard and constant work whatever the luck was, the sum in the

savings bank slowly increased ; and at last Rob
announced to his companions that they had
saved enough to enable him to purchase a share
in Coll MacDougall's boat. Neil and Duncan
and Nicol were sorely disinclined to part with
Rob ; but yet they saw clearly enough that he
was getting too old to remain at the cuddy-
fishing, and they knew they could now work
that line of business quite well by themselves.
What Rob said was this :

"You see it is a great chance for all of us
that I should get a share in the boat ; for what
I make at the herring-fishing will go into the
bank along with what you make at the trawling
by the shore. And who knows, if we all work
hard enough, who knows but we may have a
herring-skiff all to ourselves some day ? And
that would be a fine thing to have a herring-skiff
to ourselves, and our own nets ; and all that we
earned our own, and not in debt to any one
whatever."

Of course that was a dream of the future ; for
a herring-skiff costs a considerable sum of money,
and so do nets. But in the meantime they
were all agreed that what Rob counselled was
wise ; and a share in Coll MacDougall's boat was

accordingly purchased, after a great deal of bargaining.

A proud lad was Rob MacNicol the afternoon he came along to the wharf to take his place in the boat that was now partly his own. His brothers and cousin were there to see him (envious a little, perhaps; but proud also, for part of their money had gone to buy the share). He had likewise purchased second-hand a huge pair of boots that were as soft and pliable as grease could make them; and he carried a brand-new yellow oilskin in his hand that crackled as he walked. Neil, Duncan, and Nicol watched him throw his oilskin into the boat, and go forward to the bow, and take his place there at the oar; and they knew very well that if there was any one who could pull a huge oar better than Rob MacNicol, it was not in Erisaig that that person was to be found. Then the big herring-skiff passed away out to the point in the red glow of the evening; and Rob had achieved the first great ambition of his life.

CHAPTER V.

THE HIGH ROAD.

THAT was not a very good year for the herring-fishing on this part of the coast: but at all events Rob MacNicol learned all the lore of the fishermen, and grew as skilled as any of them in guessing at the whereabouts of the herring; while at the end of the season he had more than replaced the £12 he had used of the common fund. Then he returned to the tailor's boat, and worked with his brothers and cousin. He was proud to know that he had a share in a fishing-skiff; but he was not too proud to turn his hand to anything else that might help.

These MacNicol boys had grown to be greatly respected in Erisaig. The audacity of four " wastrel laddies " setting up to be fishermen on their own account had at first amused the neighbours; but their success and their conduct generally, soon raised them above

ridicule; and the women especially were warm
in their commendation. They saw how Rob
gradually improved the appearance of his
brothers and cousin. All of them had boots and
stockings now. Not only that, but they had
white shirts and jackets of blue cloth to go to
church with on Sunday; and each of them put
twopence in the collection-plate just as if they
had all been sons of a rich shopkeeper. Moreover, they were setting an example to the other
boys about. Four of these, indeed, combined to
start a cuddy-fishing business similar to that of
Rob's. Neil was rather angry; but Rob was
not afraid of any competition. He asked the
new boys to come and see how he had rigged up
the guy-poles. He said there were plenty of
fish in the sea; and the market was large
enough. But when the new boys asked him to
lend them some money to buy ropes he distinctly
declined. He had got on without borrowing
himself.

It was a long and dreary winter; but Nicol
had nearly finished with his schooling; and the
seine-net had been largely added to; and every
inch of it overhauled. Then the cuddy-fishing
began again; and soon Rob, who was now

nearly eighteen, and remarkably firm-set for his age, would be away after the herring.

One day, as Rob was going along the main thoroughfare of Erisaig, the banker called him into his office.

"Rob," said he, "have ye seen the skiff* at the building-yard?"

"Ay," said Rob rather wistfully, for many a time he had stood and looked at the beautiful lines of the new craft. "She's a splendid boat."

"And ye've seen the new drift-net in the shed?"

"Ay, I have that."

"Well, ye see, Rob," continued Mr. Bailie, regarding him with a good-natured look; "I had the boat built and the net bought as a kind of speculation; and I was thinking of getting a crew through from Tarbert. They say the herring are beginning to come about some of the western lochs. Now I have been hearing a good deal about you, Rob, from the neighbours. They say that you, and your brothers and cousin, are sober and diligent lads; and that you are good

---

* Though the herring-skiffs are so-called, they are comparatively large and powerful boats, and will stand a heavy sea.

seamen, and careful. Then you have been a while at the herring-fishing yourself. Now, do you think you could manage that new boat?"

"Me!" said Rob, with his eyes staring and his face aflame.

"I go by what the neighbours say, Rob. They say ye are a prudent lad, not over venturesome; and I think I could trust my property to ye. What say ye?"

In his excitement at the notion of being made master of such a beautiful craft, Rob forgot the respect he ought to have shown in addressing so great a person as the banker. He blurted out—

"Man, I would just like to try!"

"I will pay ye a certain sum per week while the fishing lasts," continued Mr. Bailie, "and ye will hire what crew ye think fit. Likewise I will give ye a percentage on the takes. Will that do?"

Rob was quite bewildered. All he could say was—

"I am obliged to ye, sir. Will ye wait for a minute till I see Neil?"

And very soon the wild rumour ran through Erisaig that no other than Rob MacNicol had been appointed master of the new skiff, the

Mary of Argyle, and that he had taken his
brothers and cousin as his crew. Some of the
women shook their heads; and said it was a
shame to let such mere lads go to the herring-
fishing—for some night or other they would be
drowned; but the men, who knew something of
Rob's seamanship, had no fear at all; and their
only doubt was about the younger lads being up
to the heavy work of hauling in the nets in the
morning.

But their youth was a fault that would mend
week by week. In the meantime Rob, having
sold out his share in MacDougall's boat, bought
jerseys and black boots and yellow oil-skins for
his companions; so that the new crew, if they
were rather slightly built, looked smart enough
as they went down to the slip to overhaul the
Mary of Argyle.

With what a. pride they regarded the long
and shapely lines of her—the yellow beams
shining with varnish; the tall mast at the bow,
with its stout cordage; the brand-new stove,
that was to boil their tea for them in the long
watches of the night; the magnificent oars; the
new sheets and sails—everything spick and ·
span. And this great mass of ruddy netting

lying in the shed, with its perfect floats and accurate sinkers—this was not like the make-shift that had captured the cuddies.

Then on the morning that the *Mary of Argyle* put to sea on her trial trip, her owner was on board; but he merely sat on a thwart. It was Rob who was at the tiller; Rob wanted to try the boat; the owner wanted to observe the crew. And first of all she sailed lightly out of the harbour, with the wind on her beam; then outside, the breeze being fresher, they let her away down Loch Scrone, with the brilliant new lug-sail bellying out; then they brought her round, and fought her up against the stiff wind —Rob's brief words of command being obeyed with the rapidity of lightning.

"Well, what do ye think of her?" said Mr. Bailie to his young skipper.

Rob's face was aglow with pride.

"I think she's like a race-horse!" he said. "I think she would lick any boat in Erisaig Bay."

"But it is not to run races I have handed her over to ye. You must be careful, Rob; and run back if there's any squally weather about. I'll no be vexed if you're over cautious. For ye know if anything was to happen to one of they lads, the people would say I had done wrong in lippening * a boat to such a young crew."

" Well, sir," said Rob, boldly, " ye have seen them work the boat. Do they look like lads who do not know what sailing a boat is ? "

Mr. Bailie laughed, and said no more.

Then came the afternoon on which they were to set out for the first time after the herring. All Erisaig came out to see ; and Rob was a proud lad as he stepped on board (with the lazy indifference of the trained fisherman very well imitated) and took his seat as stroke oar. The afternoon was lovely ; there was not a breath of wind ; the setting sun shone over the bay ; and the *Mary of Argyle* went away across the shining waters with the long white oars dipping with the precision of clock-work. It was not until they were at the mouth of the harbour that something occurred which seemed likely to turn this brave setting-out into ridicule.

This was Daft Sandy, who rowed his punt right across the path of the *Mary of Argyle*, and, as she came up, called to Rob.

" What is it ye want ? " Rob called to him.

* *Lippening*—trusting.

" I want to come on board, Rob," the old man said, as he now rowed his punt up to the stern of the skiff.

" I have no tobacco, and I have no whisky," Rob said impatiently. " There'll be no tobacco or whisky on board this boat so long as I have anything to do with her; so ye needna come for that, Sandy."

" It's no for that," said Daft Sandy, as, with the painter of his boat in one hand, he gripped the stern of the skiff with the other.

Now Rob was angry. Many of the Erisaig people would still be watching their setting-out; and was it to be supposed that they had taken this doited old body as one of the crew? But then Daft Sandy was at this moment clambering into the boat; and Rob could not get up and fight with an old man, who would probably tumble into the water.

" Rob," said he, in a whisper, as he fastened the painter of his punt, " I promised I would tell ye something. I'll show ye how to find the herring."

" You !" said Rob derisively.

" Ay, me, Rob, I'll make a rich man of you. I will tell you something about the herring that

not any one in Erisaig knows—that not any one
in Scotland knows."

"Why havena ye made a rich man of
yourself, Sandy?" said Rob, with more good-
nature.

The half-witted creature did not seem to see
the point of this remark.

"Ay, ay," he said, "many is the time I was
thinking of telling this one or telling that one;
but when I would go near it was always 'Daft
Sandy!' and 'Daft Sandy!' and there was
always the peltin' wi' the broken herring—
except from you, Rob. And I was saying to
myself that when Rob MacNicol has a boat of
his own, then I will show him how to find the
herring, and no one will know but himself."

By this time the MacNicols had taken to
their oars again; and they had pulled outside
the harbour, the old punt still astern. Then
Rob had to speak plainly.

"Look here, Sandy, I will not put ye ashore
by force. But I canna have your punt at the
stern of the boat. It'll be in the way of the
nets."

But the old man was more eager than ever.
If they would only pull into the bay hard by,

he would anchor the punt and leave it. He begged Rob to take him for that night's fishing. He had discovered a sure sign of the presence of herring—unknown to any of the fishermen. What was the phosphorescence in the sea ?—the nights were too clear for that. What was the mere breaking of the water ?—a moving shoal that might escape. But this sign that the old man had discovered went to show the presence of large masses of the fish, stationary and deep : it was the appearance on the surface of the water of small air-bubbles. He was sure of it. He had watched it. It was a secret worth a bankful of money. And again, he besought Rob to let him accompany him ; Rob had stopped the lads when they were throwing herring at him ; Rob alone should have the benefit of this valuable discovery of his.

Rob MacNicol was doubtful ; for he had never heard of this thing before ; but he could not resist the importunities of the old half-witted creature. They pulled in and anchored the punt ; then they set forth again, rowing slowly as the light faded out of the sky, and keeping a watch all around on the almost glassy seas.

There was no sign of any herring ; no solan

geese sweeping down; no breaking of the
water; and none of the other boats, so far as
they could make out, had as yet shot their nets.
The night was coming on, and they were far
away from Erisaig; but still old Sandy kept up
his watch, studying the surface of the water, as
if he expected to find pearls floating there.
And at last, in great excitement, he grasped
Rob's arm. Leaning over the side of the boat
they could just make out in the dusk a great
quantity of minute air-bubbles rising to the
surface of the sea.

"Put some stones along with the sinkers,
Rob," the old man said in a whisper, as if he
were afraid of the herring hearing; "go deep,
deep, deep."

Well, they quietly let out the seemingly in-
terminable drift-net as they pulled gently along,
and when that was accomplished they took in
the long oars again. Nicol lit up the little
stove, and proceeded to boil the tea. The
bundle containing their supper was opened, and
Sandy had his share and his can of tea like the
others.

They had a long time of waiting to get over
through the still summer night, but still Rob

was strangely excited, wondering whether Sandy
had really, in pottering about, discovered a new
indication of the whereabouts of the herring, or
whether he was to go back to Erisaig in the
morning with empty nets. There was another
thing too. Had he shown himself too credulous
before his companions? Had he done right in
listening to what might be only a foolish tale?
The others began to doze off; Rob not. He did
not sleep a wink all night.

Well, to let out a long drift-net, which sometimes goes as deep as fifteen fathoms, is an easy
affair, but to haul it in again is a sore task; and
when it happens to be laden, and heavily-laden,
with silver-gleaming fish, that is a break-back
business for four young lads. But there is such
a thing as the nervous, eager, joyous strength of
success; and if you are hauling in yard after
yard of a dripping net, only to find the brown
meshes all bestarred with the silver herring,—
then even young lads can work like men. Daft
Sandy was laughing all the while.

"Rob, my man, what think ye o' the air-
bubbles now? Maybe Daft Sandy is no sae
daft. And do you think I would be going and
telling any one but yourself, Rob? Do you

think I would be going and telling any one that was throwing the broken herring at me, and always a curse for me when I went near the skiffs, and not once a glass of whisky for an old man ? Well, Rob, I will not ask you for a glass of whisky. If you say it is a teetotal boat, it is a teetotal boat ; but you will not forget to give me whole herring for bait when you are going out of the bay ? "

Rob could not speak ; he was breathless. Nor was their work nearly done when they had got in the net with all its splendid gleaming treasure. There was not a breath of wind ; they had to set to work to pull the heavy boat back to Erisaig. The gray of the dawn gave way to a glowing sunrise ; when they at length reached the quay, dead-beat with fatigue and want of sleep, the people were all about.

They were dead-beat ; but there were ten crans of herring in that boat. And you should have seen Rob's air when he counselled Neil and Duncan and Nicol to go away home and have a sleep, and when he loftily called on two or three of the boys on the quay to come in and strip the nets. But the three MacNicols were far too excited to go away. They wanted to see the great heap of fish ladled out in baskets on to the quay. Mr. Bailie came along not long after that, and shook hands with Rob, and congratulated him ; for it turned out that while not another Erisaig boat had that night got more than from two to three crans, the *Mary of Argyle* had turned ten crans—as good herring as ever were got out of Loch Scrone.

Well, the MacNicol lads were now in a fair way of earning an independent and honourable living, and this sketch of how they had struggled into that position from being mere wastrels— living about the shore like so many curlews—may fitly cease here. Sometimes they had good luck, and sometimes bad luck ; but always they had the advantage of that additional means of discovering the whereabouts of the herring that had been imparted to them by Daft Sandy. And the last that the present writer heard of them was this, that they had bought outright the *Mary of Argyle* and her nets from the banker ; and that they were building for themselves a small stone cottage on the slope of the hill above Erisaig ; and that Daft Sandy had been taken away from the persecution of the harbour boys to become a sort of general major-domo—

cook, gardener, and mender of nets. Moreover, each of the MacNicols has his separate bank account now ; each has got a silver watch ; and Rob was saying the other day that he thought that he and his brothers and his cousin ought to take a trip to London (as soon as the herring-fishing was over), for perhaps they might see the Queen there, and at any rate they could go and have a look at Smithfield, where the English beheaded Sir William Wallace.

THE BLACK BOTHY.

A HIGHLAND TALE.

THE BLACK BOTHY.

A HIGHLAND TALE.

CHAPTER I.

DONNACHA RUA.

ONE warm and golden evening in August a young lad was standing at the door of a wayside cottage in one of the most remote and mountainous districts in Inverness-shire, and he was watching a slow-moving cloud of dust, which, in the distance, told of a flock of sheep being driven up from the plains below to seek pasturage in those alpine solitudes. All at once he turned and quickly went into the house.

"Mother," said he, "I know it is my uncle that is coming this time. I can see the white collie. I am sure it is my uncle this time."

The woman who sat in the high-backed wooden chair by the empty fireplace seemed too

M 2

ill to heed.   The pale, emaciated face was quite
listless and hopeless, and her hands lay idly in
her lap.

"It is a poor house he will find us in this
year," she said, without raising her head.
"There is neither bite nor sup for him."

"It is not that he will be thinking of," said
the lad; and then he added : "You know well,
mother, there might be both bite and sup if you
would let me go away to Glasgow, to work like
the others."

"I am too ill," she said, with the excusable
petulance of an invalid.   "I am too ill, Andrew.
Ye mustna think of going away to Glasgow yet."

Andrew Ross did not stay to urge the point,
for he thought the best thing he could do was to
go away along the road and meet his uncle, and
tell him how matters stood.   There would be
little enough time, for Donnacha Rua—that is
Red Duncan—was taking these sheep up to the
wilds of Allt-nam-bà, some half a dozen miles
farther on, and his visit to his sister-in-law in
the little cottage was likely to be of the briefest.

"Well, Andrew," said the tall red-bearded
shepherd, when the lad drew near, "and how is
your mother now?"

" She is out of the fever," said Andrew Ross ;
" but still she is very ill. But it is no wonder.
The doctor says she is to have better food. But
where are we to get better food ? It is to Glasgow that I am thinking of going, to work like
the others, and then I could send money to my
mother and Maggie. But my mother says no,
and Maggie she begins to cry ; and what am I
to do ? "

" I was hearing they would not be wanting
you on the hill this year," his uncle said.

" No, nor at the kennels either ; for Big
Murdoch brought two or three strange lads with
him in the spring. But this year they will want
no gillies whatever. Did you not hear that the
grouse round about here had all been killed with
the disease ? "

" Yes, I was hearing that too."

" It is a bad thing for us, uncle. There are
none of the gentry coming up this year, and the
lodges are all empty—every one of them between
here and Corrievreak, and so my mother sent
away the lass that helped her with the washing.
And what are we to do now, if I do not go away
to Glasgow, or to Greenock ? The schoolmaster
says I could get a good place. I have learned

book-keeping by double entry, and now it is no use my stopping here, as long as Big Murdoch has the charge at Etherick Lodge."

He was clearly anxious to get away, and doubtless not without some hope that his uncle would approve of the step; but at this moment they arrived at the cottage, and nothing further could be said.

The big red-bearded shepherd posted his sagacious collies so that the sheep should not stray too far, and then went indoors.

"It is not the best news I have heard, Christina," said he, sitting down and taking out his pipe, but not lighting it. "But when things are at their worst, they maun mend."

"I do not see how they are to mend," said this sickly-looking woman, in dejected and hopeless fashion. "There will be no one at Etherick Lodge this year. I sent away the young lass that used to help me with the washing. It was but another mouth to feed."

"Where is wee Maggie?" he asked, to vary the subject.

"She is out herding the cow. That is the last thing that belongs to us; and I suppose we will have to sell that."

Tears began to trickle down her cheeks. It was clear that the illness from which she was recovering had left her in a state of extreme nervous depression and despair, and that she was not at all in a condition to face the very actual and literal troubles of the hour.

"Come, come, Christina," the big shepherd said, cheerfully, "it's no so bad as that. You'll no have to sell the coo as long as Andrew here has a pair of willing hands to work wi'. You'll just have to make the best o' things, as other folks have had to do; and the first thing is to get back a little o' your strength. That is what is the matter with ye—a kind o' weakness, I can see; and I was hearing that the doctor was recommending ye to have some better food. You're ower white-faced, woman. There will be no much chance for ye to fight the battle o' the world on a little oatmeal, and I suppose that is all there is in the house?"

She did not answer; and he knew he had guessed the truth.

"Well, now, Christina," he continued, "here is Andrew willing to go away to Glasgow."

She shook her head.

"Not yet; not yet," she said, feebly. "Let

him wait till the end. It will no be long. My days are numbered——"

"Toots! toots! woman," he said, impatiently. "Are you going to leave the bairns to fight their way by themselves? Is that like a wise woman? What you have to do is to get back some o' your strength, and then you'll be in a better state to say what Andrew maun do, and your head will be clearer. I suppose now," said he, regarding her thin, pinched face, "if Lord Etherick were at the Lodge, he might be sending you a hare now and again?"

"Many's the hare he used to send me," the widow woman said, "and her ladyship too. When Maggie was ill, it was one thing or another she was always sending—even a picture-book for her to look at. But this year there is no one at the Lodge—no one at all; and it would be waiting many a day before Big Murdoch would think of doing any one a kindness."

"I do not see why we should be beholden to Big Murdoch, or to any one else, mother," said Andrew Ross. "Let me go to Glasgow, and get a good wage. What is it here, even if John Malcolm were to come back and give me a place? For driving the woods, a shilling a day.

and when I was at the kennels, another six shillings a week. What is that? I am not afraid to go to Glasgow."

And here, to his amazement, his uncle interposed with a sullen and definite negative.

"No, no, Andrew, my lad. It is no use distressing your mother. Wait till she is better —wait till she is stronger—then you can see what is to be done."

He rose.

"Good-bye, Christina. I will be hearing of you from time to time, when any of the shepherds are coming up to Allt-nam-ba. And if any bit present—do ye understand?—should reach ye from the hills—a hare or two, maybe, or something like that—just you take them, and use them, and say nothing about them; and I hope by the next time I see ye, you'll no have such a white face."

As he was going out, he quietly touched his nephew on the shoulder; and the lad understood, and followed.

"Andrew, my lad," said he, when they were outside, "I have something to say to ye—ye can walk along the road with me for a bit. Your mother is ill; and I'm thinking the doctor is right—she'll no be much stronger till she gets something better to eat than a pickle oatmeal. It's a great pity that his lordship's family is no coming up the year; and there'll be no shooting; and the hares on the tops up there just running about in such numbers that it's a sin and a shame to see them, and to think there are sick folk in the country that a potful o' hare-soup would be a kind o' providence to. Ay, ay."

The tall and stalwart shepherd, as he stalked along after his flock, seemed cautious in his speech; and yet there was a humorous twinkle in his eye.

"Now, Andrew," said he, "if a body were to put his hand on one or two o' they hares— there's far too many of them for the ground, and if they do not thin them down there will come a murrain among them, as a sensible keeper would know—and if they were put somewhere where they could be found, to be taken down to your mother, and for her to say nothing, but to make use o' them, and put some life into the poor woman, do ye think you know of a smart lad anywhere who would come up to Allt-nam-ba, and find the place I could tell him of, and make

his way back in the dusk without letting Big
Murdoch or any of them see him?"

Andrew Ross understood at once, and his eyes
lit up at the prospect of this adventure. There
were several reasons that made him willing to
undertake it. It was not only that his mother
was ill, and that this addition to their scanty
supply of food would be of inestimable value to
her; but also, among other things, it would give
him an opportunity of outwitting Big Murdoch,
who, succeeding to John Malcolm, had brought
his own gillies with him, and had thus deprived
two or three of the lads about there of their
occupation, and who was known to be of such a
jealous and grudging disposition that he would
have prosecuted a starving crofter for picking
up a stray rabbit.

"I would come up myself," said the lad
boldly, "at any time you like, and at any hour
of the night you like."

"There's better than a hare," said the red
shepherd, after a minute or two. "If I could
get a fine young roebuck, that would be a better
thing; and many's the good meal you could
make of one for a weakly woman. Sometimes
there are a few roe in the woods at Allt-nam-ba;

and what would be the harm to take one, when there is no one shooting, and all the roe going away again before the winter? Andrew, my lad, could you carry a roe from Allt-nam-ba over the hills to your home?"

"Indeed I could try," said the other, "and I should not be afraid to try. But how are you going to get a roe, uncle, when you have no gun?"

Red Duncan, without saying anything, took out a bit of string from his pocket; and in a second or two had fitted up, in miniature, a clever running noose.

"Do you see that, Andrew? All that you want is to know their track; and if you have the line just a little below the level of their head, and wide enough, and well hidden among the young larches, in he goes, and the more he struggles the faster he is."

"Give me the chance, and you will see whether I can carry him or not," said young Ross. "And my mother, she will be having her dinner every day, like the Queen at Balmoral, for a week or a fortnight after that."

"Well, then, I will tell you, Andrew; but it is very cautious you must be; for Big Murdoch is a hard man, and many's the one he has

summoned for taking less than a roe. Do you
know the little swinging bridge where the Allt-
crôm comes down ? "

" Well I know it."

" Very well, if you go over the bridge and
cross a strip of bog, there is a small gully there
that leads up to the moor above. Do you know
it ? "

" Oh, very well."

" Then you know the rocks at the top of the
gully, I am sure of that. Now, this is Tuesday
night; on Thursday night, the night after to-
morrow, Andrew, you will go over the hills—I
am sure you know the way as well as anyone
—keeping out of sight of Etherick altogether;
and you will cross over the bridge and go up
the rocks, and not until the sun is about to go
down. Maybe you will find something there;
maybe a hare or two, maybe a roe, maybe a
small piece of paper telling you to wait a little
until it is darker, and then you will know I am
bringing something, and they may be following
you, for Big Murdoch is after every one that
comes up the glen. You will mind that, now.
You will keep away from the glen—back among
the hills, until you come down to the water;

and if you cross over by the stones instead of by the bridge, that will be better still. Do you think you can manage it ? "

" Indeed, I am sure I can manage it, uncle, if you can manage the catching of the roe."

" Maybe it will be a roe, and maybe not," said the red shepherd, " for it is a short time; but any one that would be seeing your mother would be a hard man if he was grudging her a roe or a hare or two until the illness has left her. Indeed, I am sure if his lordship was at Etherick this year, there would be no need for you and for me to be setting about this thing for ourselves, and all the time afraid of Big Murdoch and the strange gillies."

Shortly after this Andrew Ross bade good-night to his uncle, and set out on his return homeward, sufficiently impressed with the seriousness of what he had undertaken and yet not over-dismayed. For one thing, there were few in that neighbourhood who knew it better, or were better fitted for an enterprise of the kind. Every sinuous water-course, every lonely cairn and chasm, was familiar to him; and if his uncle was not afraid to take the risk of snaring this roe-deer, he, on his part, was not going to shrink from the task of carrying it home across the hills.

It is true he would rather have done that—had it been possible—in the daylight. There are many superstitions still existing in that part of the country—dark traditions of water-kelpies and other ghostly creatures that are supposed to wander away in the night-time from the lakes, which are their proper habitations. Loch Etherick was known to be haunted by a black horse—or an animal resembling a horse—which on more than one occasion according to popular belief, had been encountered among the neighbouring hills; and it was across those very hills that young Ross had to make his way back in the dark. However, he was a sensible and shrewd-headed lad, and he contented himself with thinking that the actual labour and fatigue of carrying a roebuck some five or six miles would be quite enough to drive imaginary terrors out of his brain. And who could tell but that this poor widow woman, nourished by this more solid and substantial food, might get into a more cheerful and hopeful condition, and might be willing to see him start away on his adventurous journey to Glasgow, now that Big

Murdoch and the grouse disease together had deprived him of occupation in his native glen?

Next day while attending to the various duties demanded by the small patch of ground attached to the cottage, he also managed to rig up a piece of mechanism, consisting of a bent piece of wood and a double coil of stout rope. This—whether his uncle should secure two or three mountain hares or a roebuck—would enable him to carry the precious booty all the more easily across the hills.

And then again the next afternoon—and not without some little tremor of anxiety, though he whistled loudly and cheerfully as long as his small sister Maggie was within hearing—he set out to keep his tryst; and after many subtle and sinuous wanderings through solitary glens, along stony mountain-slopes, and by the sides of brawling streams, he at length reached the cairn of stones at the top of the gully that his uncle had described; and here he found himself the sole inhabitant of the wilderness lying all around him, just as the dusk of a rather cloudy and stormy and troubled day was about to fall over the lonely landscape.

CHAPTER II.

A RETREAT.

THE first glance round his hiding-place had shown him that neither roe nor hares had been left for him there by his uncle; but it was not until his eyes had got accustomed to his surroundings—to this little dell of boulders, and bracken, and heather, that he observed, on the top of one of the stones, a tiny piece of folded paper. This he instantly opened; and found written on it the single word " *Wait.*" Then he understood. No doubt his uncle had been successful, and was only allowing the daylight to wane still further, for safety's sake, before bringing the game to Andrew Ross's place of concealment. There was nothing for it but to obey in patience that monosyllabic injunction.

And yet, despite himself, the lad grew anxious and restless. It was a wild-looking evening. Every minute the gusts that came tearing down

N

from the mountain ravines, to go howling along the empty glens below, seemed to increase in force, and there was every promise of a tempestuous night. No doubt, he said to himself, if he were struggling under the load of a roebuck, or some three or four mountain hares—and having, besides, the roughest of country to get over at the same time—this nervousness would disappear; but, in the meantime, it must be confessed he did not feel at all comfortable, and again and again he impatiently peered over the boulders—only to find before him the same stretch of heathery hillside leading away,down to a ravine, where the swollen waters of the Allt-crôm were noisily brawling.

Then suddenly, in this gloomy twilight, he made out in the distance the figure of a man, coming rapidly along by the outskirts of the young birch trees that fringed the side of the ravine. It was the figure of a tall man, and he seemed to be carrying something slung over his shoulder. Another second or two of anxious observation, and now the lad Ross knew for certain that this was his uncle, and was almost convinced that he was bringing a roebuck. Then all his nervousness vanished. He bethought him only of the hard fight across the hills under the heavy weight. He was anxious to get away before the darkness of night came on ; once up on the hills above the loch, he would be able to find his way right enough. Nor did he stop to ask himself whether this roe-buck which was now being brought him did not belong, strictly and morally, to Lord Etherick ; and, indeed, that was a question that might have puzzled a more able casuist, for, in these alti-tudes, the roe-deer are mere fleeting summer visitors, sometimes remaining in the woods for only a day or two, sometimes for a month or two, but always returning to their homes in the lower valleys before the coming winter.

Red Duncan was now coming rapidly yet cautiously on, keeping always by the birch-trees, so that he should not be observed from the other side of the glen. Andrew had got his coil of rope prepared ; he was ready to sling the deer over his shoulders at a moment's notice. Sud-denly there was a sharp whistle that sounded strangely distant, even in the howling of these mountain gusts. He saw his uncle stop and look behind him. At the same moment, to his inexpressible alarm—he beheld two figures

emerge from the thicket of birch-trees, clambering up into the open, and he heard one of them
call out, in loud and bantering tones :

" Not so fast ; you will be soon enough in
Inverness gaol ! "

The wind was blowing towards him ; he heard
the rancorous tones of the man's voice, and well
he knew the voice to be the voice of Big
Murdoch.   With his heart beating with fear and
apprehension he lay down among the rocks and
bushes—never hare lay closer.   He scarcely
dared to breathe.   If they were to discover him,
that would only make the evidence against Red
Duncan more complete ; he kept wondering to
himself whether they had seen him peering over
the edge of the boulders—whether they were
now running towards him.   But time passed,
and he heard nothing.   The blasts of wind that
were howling over his head brought no other
sound.   Had the keeper and the gillie returned
down the glen, then, satisfied with the results of
their watching ? and had his uncle gone away
back to the hillside, with the knowledge that
soon a summons for day-poaching would be out
against him ?   Andrew Ross raised his head a
little bit, and listened intently.   Then he ven-

tured a little farther—until at length, with the
greatest caution, he could just look over the
edge of one of the boulders. There was no one
there. The gloomy and darkening landscape
was empty. Finally, having assured himself
that the coast was clear, he slipped out of his
hiding-place, made his way down through the
bushes by which he had come up, waded knee-
deep across the stream rather than make himself
conspicuous by crossing the foot-bridge, and with
such speed as was possible—for a kind of terror
haunted him—followed the windings of the
stream until, in the deepening gloom, he could
vaguely make out before him the wide waters of
Loch Etherick.

And yet it was not any terror for himself that
haunted him, it was the dread of what might
happen to his uncle. Would they take him to
the county police office at Inverness? would
they interview him in the gaol—in the great red
building that is known as the Castle? would his
name be in the newspapers, so that every one
should know? And all this shame to befall him
because he had taken pity on a poor widow
woman—his own sister-in-law. But all this adventure now looked different in the eyes of the

lad Ross.   He had been excited by the risk and
danger of it.   He had looked forward with pride
to telling his mother and his sister Maggie that
now there was a store of food in the house, and
they might have a dinner fit for a queen.   But
all this was gone now.   There was nothing but
shame and exposure.   And it seemed hard that
his uncle's good-nature should have brought this
trouble on him.   What would his master,
Colonel Graham, say?   Would he keep in his
employment a man who had been convicted of
poaching?   And there was no doubt that Big
Murdoch would take out the summons—not the
least.   If John Malcolm had been still at
Etherick Lodge, some intercession might have
been possible.   Donnacha Rua might have been
let off with a warning.   But Big Murdoch had
always gone to the severest extremes, and his
name was of evil omen in the neighbourhood.
And then Etherick Lodge was empty this year,
otherwise his mother might have pleaded with
her ladyship, and told her that it was not for
himself that Red Duncan had snared the roe.
The more he looked at it, the more did Ross's
heart sink within him, and he thought he never
would be able to hold up his head again if he

were to see his own uncle taken away into Inverness by a couple of policemen.

These anxious and troubled forebodings were all at once startled out of his head by a more immediate peril. Right in front of him, though still at some distance, in the middle of the path skirting the edge of the loch, stood the Etherick bull. There was no mistaking him for any water-kelpie or other ghostly creature, dark as the night was. He knew the beast too well. It was the terror of the country-side—an ill-tempered brute, that cared not for any obstacles once its anger was aroused. And now young Ross paused, peering through the gloom at this animal, and trying to make out whether it was disposed to advance and stop his way, or whether he might try to slip by it unobserved. Of one thing he was certain. If the beast happened to be in an ill-temper, it was no use his taking to the steep hillside, for the bull was as active as a roe. His only safety was in the water—supposing him to have time to run down and jump into the boat which usually lay moored at this end of the loch.

He had not the opportunity of thinking twice. With a slow muttering, rather than any roaring,

the beast slowly advanced. There was nothing
for it but immediate flight. Fortunately the
boat was quite close by, at a small, rude,
landing-quay built of stone, and a very few
seconds indeed were sufficient for him to reach
the mooring-post, throw off the iron chain, and
leap into the boat. The bull had not, as he
expected, charged him. It had merely come
sulkily and threateningly onward; and when
at last he managed to shove off the boat into
deeper water, the animal was down at the side
of the loch, still regarding him, and muttering
and growling, as it were. He took no more
heed of it. His immediate business was with
the boat, which was rapidly drifting away before
the fierce squalls of wind which came scouring
down the glen. Indeed, before he had got the
oars fixed in their places, and was trying to get
the bow of the boat round, he found that he
had drifted well out into the loch, the almost
unseen waters of which were now driven and
lashed by the gale.

This Loch Etherick was a small loch—some
two miles long by half a mile broad—and his
first rapid thought, when he was driven to take
refuge in the boat by the advance of the bull,

was that he would row along the shore until he
was out of sight of the animal, then land, and
fasten the boat to any rock that might be handy.
The boat belonged to Etherick Lodge, and some
of the people there would be sure to see it in
the morning, and would doubtless take it back
to the proper moorings. But very speedily he
found that it was not where he wished that the
boat was going, but where those sharp and
sudden hurricanes were driving it—and that was
right over to the other shore. Do what he
could, it was impossible for him to fight against
these squalls. Sometimes there was a lull—
indeed, he had made some good progress in the
direction he was aiming for—though it was now
so dark he could scarcely see either shore ; and
then again another whirl of the gale would come
sweeping down the glen, and away he would go
helpless. Moreover, he knew there was no path
along the other side of the loch. The hills there
came sheer down into the water ; in one or two
places they overhung the loch in projecting
crags. If he were to land, his only chance of
getting home that night would be to climb a
mountain-side about as steep as the side of a
house, and then take the risk of finding his way

across the Etherick deer forest. So, again and again he put the bow of the boat against the heavy wind-squalls, and fought and fought as best he could, and again and again he found himself beaten and driven back by the wind. Besides this, he had not the strength with which he began : his arms were aching, his back was like to break. To crown all, it was now so dark that he could not see across the loch ; and to be out on this sheet of black water at this time of night, with a hurricane roaring and shrieking around, was far from being comfortable, and so at last he yielded to circumstances, and allowed the wind to drive the boat before it, until she suddenly and noisily crashed on to some stones ; then, in almost pitch blackness, he jumped out into the water, and tugged and hauled at the boat until he had got the bow well up on the shore, and finally he got the chain and wound that twice round a boulder of rock, making everything as secure as he knew how. He had then to consider his own position.

It was not a pleasant one. If there had been any glimpse of starlight or moonlight to show him his surroundings, that might have helped him somewhat ; but at present he only knew

that behind him was the loch, and before him
the steep side of the hill, without any path or
track, and covered with loose blocks of granite,
which at any moment might give way beneath
his feet, and cause him to go hurling down an
unknown depth. He thought of trying the boat
again, but his arms were now powerless. That
was useless. Then he wondered whether it
would not be better to grope his way to some
big granite boulder, and lie down under the lee
of that until the light of the morning should
show him some way out of his perplexities. But
then again he knew his mother and the little
Maggie would be dreadfully alarmed by his not
coming home, and would make sure that he had
perished in the storm ; and so, at all hazards, he
resolved to try to get to the top of this steep
hillside. Once on the soft moss and heather of
the deer forest he felt sure he would be able
to make his way somehow, for he knew this
mountainous district well, and had many a
time before had to make his way home in the
dark.

Then he bethought him of a small river-course
that he knew well enough from seeing it from
the other side of the loch. In summer this was

little more than a steeply-ascending mass of dry
stones, with some small channels of water
trickling through. Now, he thought, if he could
only make his way to this water-course, would it
not lead him up to some corrie above, by which
his way to the top would be made more easy?
It was, at all events, the only thing he could
think of doing in the extremity of the moment;
and he set about it forthwith. He groped his
way along the shore, stumbling over the stones,
and always feeling for some boggy bunches of
grass to tell him where the rivulet came down.
These he speedily found, discovering that he was
up to the ankles and over in marshy and spongy
holes; and so at once he set to work to climb,
almost hand over hand, up the rough water-
course. He got pretty wet, and his knees and
shins received a sufficient number of bruises;
but always he had the notion in his head that,
once on the top, in the open deer forest, there
would be some faint starlight to enable him to
see his way. As he went on he found that this
water-course retreated into a small glen. It
was easier going now; but also it was much
darker; and he had to get over whatever
obstacles came in his way blindly enough—

granite blocks, bushes, or splashing little water-
falls. He was soaked through now, partly with
the wet from without, partly from perspiration ;
but he fought on courageously, squirming up
this little ravine like some wild animal ; and
constantly wondering whether any human being
had ever been in this wild place before.

Well, if that was the question he was asking
himself, it was quickly and definitely answered.
In the recesses of this little ravine there was
almost silence ; the wind seemed to go roaring
by outside of it. And it was in the half-silence,
and in the absolute darkness, that young Ross—
little thinking that human creatures could be in
his neighbourhood—suddenly heard voices. He
stopped, paralysed, not daring to move. The
voices sounded quite near, but he could see
nothing. Then all at once there was a red flash
in the blackness—it was a ray of light apparently from the other side of the chasm. A
sort of terror rooted him to the spot ; all sorts
of weird and frightful stories crowded into his
recollection ; he was trembling in every limb.
He had not self-possession enough to reflect that
the sounds he had heard were undoubtedly
human voices ; he could only crouch among the

bushes unable to stir, and almost unable to breathe ; his fascinated, fear-stricken eyes gazing on that small point of red light that burned steadily enough there in the darkness, not more than a dozen or twenty yards away from him.

CHAPTER III.

THE BOTHAN DUBH.

INDEED, the lad was far too terrified to reflect. That he should suddenly encounter human beings in this almost inaccessible chasm on the verge of the deer forest, and at this time of night, was quite as extraordinary as anything supernatural, and he kept his eyes fixed on that small point of red light with a sort of fascination of fear, dreading he knew not what, and not daring to stir hand or foot. Presently the light seemed to grow bigger—to show itself in a number of streaks, then in a wide broad glow, as if a hole had been cut in the side of the mountain, revealing a mass of fire within. Then two dark figures appeared between him and the breadth of ruddy light; and with a strange distinctness—for he was but a stone's throw away from them—he heard them speak. And surely he recognised this voice :

"Pete, my man, ye'll have to go round and bring the boat across the loch; and look sharp too. We're late the nicht; it will never do to keep the cart standing at the end of the loch, and four sacks o' malt in it too. A fine thing if some o' the supervisor's chiels were to come along the road!"

"No fears," said one of his companions— for there seemed to be three or four there. "They'd rather be in their bed on a wild night like this. Here, Sandy, just give us a hoist wi' this cask till I fasten the rope."

Again a dead silence. The dark figures were moving this way and that, engaged in some occupation or other. But now, in spite of all his terror, the lad who was crouching there could not but understand what was going on before him. He had accidentally tumbled over a *bothan dubh*—a black bothy—an illicit still; and these men seemed to be so convinced of their security in this inaccessible place that they allowed the entrance to the bothy to remain without cover or concealment while they talked openly of their affairs outside here in the dark. Probably if he had had time to think the lad would have been glad to assure himself that there was nothing of the supernatural, after all, in his immediate neighbourhood ; but he was too intent on observing what was going on, and in listening for the slightest sound. Moreover, he knew well that his own safety depended on his remaining there unperceived by them. There was at that time—and there is now—a good deal of illicit distillation going on in the county of Inverness ; and the men engaged in it were known to be rather a wild and reckless lot—though, ordinarily, when the Supervisor of Inland Revenue and his assistants of the Preventive Force made 'a raid on a mountain distillery, the owners of it preferred to show a clean pair of heels. But here, at this moment, supposing they were suddenly to discover this youth spying on them ? Andrew Ross knew that the loch was near, and the night dark. If they were to throw him in, how should one ever hear of him again ? And, indeed, it was not of his own free will that he was playing the spy. He would have given all his worldly possessions —which did not amount to much—if he could have been allowed to crawl away through the bushes unheard and unseen. That, however, was impossible. If he could hear them so

o

distinctly, in the hush of this chasm, so they would hear him if he made the slightest sound; and if he attempted to move, some loose stone or rotten branch would almost certainly betray him. There was nothing for it but to wait until the men had gone; and it was apparent that two of them, at all events, were getting ready to go.

"By the time ye've brought back the malt, Pete," said the biggest of the three men, in a voice that again struck Andrew Ross as being familiar to him, though he was too much alarmed and excited to think further about it— "I'll be waiting for ye doon at the loch side. We maun get it into the malting bothy by oursels, for it will be better for Sandy to go right on wi' the cart to Inverness."

"That's a fine long turn on a coarse night like this," said one of them, rather discontentedly.

"Why, man," said his companion, with a bantering laugh, "the wind's behind ye; it'll blow ye there in no time." And then he added, more gravely: "I'm no sure about that man Munro. He's a stupid creature, and as frightened as a hare. If a bit bairn were to ask him what

he had in the cart I believe he'd leave everything and run. I'm thinking ye'd better drive
the cart yourself, Sandy, when you're going into
Inverness ; and just whistle a bit tune, or be
smoking your pipe like, until ye get round to
the cooper's. We maun get another man than
Munro, sooner or later. For ten shillings I
believe he'd tell the whole story at the Inland
Revenue Office if once they had frichtened him.
Keep an eye on him, Sandy—keep an eye on
him ! It would be a fine thing if all our gear was
to be seized—the new mash-tin and everything."

"Ay, and that would be the least o't,
Murdoch, for you and for us, too. I'm thinking
his lordship wouldna be long in gieing us notice
to quit."

This word "Murdoch" threw a new light on
the affair. Yes, there could be no doubt that
the biggest of these three men was Murdoch, the
head keeper. And Sandy, too, and Pete ; he
knew these as the names of two of the gillies—
two of the strange gillies whom Murdoch had
brought with him. And so it was to Murdoch
that the black bothy belonged ? And this was
the trade he was carrying on when the gentry
were not at Etherick for the shooting ?

"Are you ready, Pete?" said one of the gillies.

"I am."

"Gang on first, then; and take care o' your neck. I'll take my time and wait for ye to bring round the boat. Good-night to ye, Murdoch."

"Good-night, Sandy. Mind what ye're about in Inverness. And tell the cooper the new mash-tin holds a hundred and twenty gallons. He'll soon be driving a roaring trade."

When the dark figures moved away from the glare of the entrance to the bothy, Andrew Ross completely lost sight of them, so dense was the surrounding darkness; but he could hear the sound of them as they set out to make their way down to the loch. He could not tell whether each of them had a small cask strapped on to his shoulders, or whether both were engaged in lowering one large barrel by means of ropes. But, at all events, they made slow progress, to judge by the noise; and for some little time the third remaining figure—doubtless that of Big Murdoch—stood at the bothy, probably listening. Then he disappeared into the glow. The light grew gradually less and less. At last there was darkness. And now, for the first time during this long and anxious half-hour, the lad who had been lying concealed there could raise himself and breathe freely.

His first and anxious thought was to get away. He had no idea as yet as to the importance of the discovery he had so accidentally made. For a minute or two he remained in suspense, wondering whether Big Murdoch might not come out again from the bothy. Then, hearing and seeing nothing, he began quietly to push his way onward and upward through the ravine, hoping at last to reach the smoother heights of the forest. In this he was in time successful. The gusts of wind that met his face occasionally told him that he was nearing a more open district, and by-and-by he made sure that he had reached the summit, and might now endeavour to steer as straight a course homeward as his guessing and knowledge of the country suggested. The night was still dark, and it was blowing hard; but he had now got amongst smooth heather and moss, and he held on his way for some considerable time, until his wandering into some bushes told him he had reached the outskirts of the long range of woods

lying between the deer forest and the valley in
which stood his mother's cottage. By working
down through these woods he could at any
moment strike the main road, so that he now
knew he was safe, and this consciousness en-
abled him to think over with a little more clear-
ness the strange things that had just occurred.

And then it suddenly flashed across his mind
that here might be the means of saving his uncle
from the shame and disgrace that threatened
him. He had no doubt whatever that it was
Big Murdoch himself who was conducting this
secret enterprise of illicit distillation, and that
was a good deal more serious crime than the
mere snaring of a roebuck. At least, so it
would appear in the eyes of Lord Etherick—
that he knew well; for his lordship had again
and again declared that he would not tolerate
the existence of any "black bothy" on his
estate, and had always been eager to give aid to
the Excise officers in their quest. But how was
he to approach Lord Etherick? How was he to
prove what he had seen? Nay, would the one
thing be held to condone the other? Even if
Big Murdoch were shown to be working an illicit
still, how would that save Red Duncan from

a summons for poaching? And what would Colonel Graham say? It would be no excuse to *him*. If Donnacha Rua were fined or imprisoned in Inverness for having snared the roe-deer, it was almost certain that Colonel Graham would no longer employ him as shepherd.

And then again young Ross remembered that he had taken away the boat from its proper moorings, and brought it to the side of the loch just under the bothy. It was pretty certain that the two gillies would find it there; indeed, whichever of them sought to go round the shores by the loch would be almost sure to stumble against it; but would not its removal suggest to them that some stranger had been there? Would they not take instant steps to remove all the distilling apparatus to some other hiding-place? There were many corries and ravines in that neighbourhood, and he had often heard how the entrance to a "black bothy" could be so cunningly hidden over with heather that the keenest eye would fail to detect it. In that case, what could he prove? This story would be no better than an old wife's tale. Nay, it would only make Big Murdoch all the more savage, and drive him to put upon Red Duncan, as far as he could, the extremest penalty of the law.

These were not cheering reflections, especially to one who considered himself as, in a measure, responsible for the calamity that was likely to overtake his uncle; but, at all events, he was soon to have one small grain of comfort vouchsafed him. He had not quite reached the road (having . struggled down through the thick underwood), when he heard in the distance the sound of the wheels of a cart. He instantly flung himself down on the heather and waited. Of course there could be only the one cart in such a lonely neighbourhood as this, and at such an hour—the cart conveying the illicit whiskey to Inverness. So he lay, face downwards, and waited and listened, and very soon, as the cart came along in the darkness, he heard the voices of two men talking in rather low tones. This greatly reassured him. It was now clear enough that they had not taken alarm at finding the boat on the wrong side of the loch. If they had, Sandy, the gillie, would undoubtedly have gone back to the bothy and reported. Instead of that, it must be he who was now talking to the carter as they trudged on together through the night, and young Ross allowed them to get on some distance ahead before he rose and followed.

Then he recollected that the Roman Catholic priest at Edenbridge had permission from Lord Etherick not only to fish in the loch, but also to use the boat when he wished ; and as his reverence was rather a portly personage, and not given to much violent exercise, he was in the habit of leaving the boat wherever was most convenient to him, on the understanding that Big Murdoch would take it back to its proper moorings when he happened to cast his eye on it. And so the gillies had had no suspicion aroused ? The "black bothy" was still to be found in that chasm, with all its apparatus of mash-tin, worm, and still. It was still possible for the Inland Revenue officers from Inverness, supposing they were led by a trusty guide, to make a sudden descent and capture not only all the spirit, but perhaps also to arrest Big Murdoch in the very midst of his illicit doings ?

"Very well, then," said Andrew Ross to himself (for the Highlander is a revengeful person where any of his family have been wronged, as history has shown before now) ; "maybe I can-

not save my uncle from being sent to Inverness.
Maybe he has to be sent to gaol because he took
pity on my mother. Perhaps I cannot help
that; but this I will make sure of—that if he
has to go to gaol, the man that sent him there
will very soon find himself there too !"

When he reached home he found his mother
still sitting up, and the poor woman was in a
dreadfully anxious and agitated state, and overwhelmed him with questions as to where he had
been, and what had kept him out on so wild a
night. But he had strength enough of mind to
keep his own counsel. He was not going to
alarm her still further by saying what had
happened to Donnacha Rua.

"I went up to see my uncle," said he, "and I
stayed until it was nearly dark, and it's a long
way over the hills on so black a night."

"A black night, indeed !" the widow woman
said. "I was thinking of waking up Maggie,
and sending her to Edenbridge to the schoolmaster; but when I went to the door I saw it
would be useless. What made you stay so late,
Andrew ?"

"Well, mother, I met the Etherick bull, and
I had to jump into the boat; and the wind was

so strong it blew me over to the other side of the loch, and I couldna get back ; so I left the boat and climbed up the hillside, and came down by the edge of the forest. It was a long way, with the night so dark."

Very soon after he got to bed, but not to sleep. The adventures of that evening had been too exciting, the possibilities of the future too alarming, to permit of that. He lay awake hour after hour, despite all the fatigue he had undergone ; and if there was one conclusion that he arrived at amidst all this turmoil of conjecture, fear, and anxiety, it was that the first thing he would do in the morning would be to go along to Edenbridge to seek counsel of the schoolmaster there. He had been the master's favourite while he was at school, and the two had remained very good friends—not to say cronies—ever since.

CHAPTER IV.

THE SCHOOLMASTER.

Long before school-time next morning he made his way to Edenbridge, and there he found the schoolmaster—a shock-headed young man of twenty-five or so—at his breakfast, which consisted of a capacious dish of oatmeal porridge. To him the lad rapidly and eagerly told all the story of his adventures of the preceding evening and night, and he had scarcely completed that when Mr. Angus bade him dismiss at least one apprehension from his mind.

"They'll no put your uncle in gaol. Ye need not fear that, anyway, Andrew, my lad. The worst will be a summons to Inverness and a fine."

"But is that no bad enough?" Andrew Ross said, almost reproachfully. "Where is he to get the money to pay the fine? And if Colonel

Graham hears of it, will he not be for sending him away ? And what is to be done then ?"

The schoolmaster finished his porridge, and rose and took a turn or two up and down the room.

" It's pretty hard," said he, " Andrew ; but the law is the law, and ye'll no get the authorities at Inverness to look on the snaring o' the roe as an act of good-nature and charity to a poor widow woman. And this that ye tell me about Big Murdoch is most extraordinar'. Your coming on the distilling bothy looks like a providential kind o' thing ; and I can see what you have been thinking about—that somebody should go and say to Big Murdoch : ' Let Duncan Ross alone for the snaring of the roe, and we will say nothing about the black bothy.' "

The lad looked eagerly at him. It was clear that some project of this kind had been in his mind. But the schoolmaster shook his head.

" That winna do, Andrew. I'm afraid it would be what the lawyers would call compounding a felony. And yet it seems hard that your uncle should be fined—and might lose his place as well—for taking a bit roe-deer that was

of no use to anybody, and that this man
Murdoch should be the prosecutor. Faith, a
fine prosecutor! A fine prosecutor, on my
word! I wonder what Lord Etherick would
say were he to learn that there was an illicit
distillery doing a splendid trade within half a
mile or so of Etherick Lodge ? "

"But, Mr. Angus," said the lad, "is there
nothing to be done to help my uncle? I am
not afraid to go to Big Murdoch. I will tell
him I know where the still is, but that I can
hold my tongue if he will say nothing about the
summons. It is a hard thing to think of—what
is going to happen to my uncle—and not be
able to do anything. It was my mother he was
trying to help; it was not for himself that he
was taking the roe."

"I understand ye well enough, Andrew, my
lad," said the schoolmaster; "but we maun
consider. Now, if ye were to go to Big Murdoch
with that fine proposition of yours, what would
happen? He would laugh, take the still to
some other place, and just flatly contradict ye
and defy ye. It would be the same as giving
him warning. Do ye think he would depend on
your holding your tongue ? Not likely."

The schoolmaster took another turn or so up and down the room. It was obvious that he was studying his own solution of this problem.

" I have no goodwill to Big Murdoch myself," said he, after a minute or two. " He was the first that ever checked me for fishing in the Etherick burns, as if it could ever have entered any human creature's head to write for permission to fish in burnlets like these ! Ay, and so this very strict person is busy day and night cheating the Excise ; and making more out o' that, I'll be sworn, than out o' his keepership. And now I understand, Andrew, why he brought the strange gillies with him, do ye see ? "

The lad was less concerned about this, though it had lost him his own employment, than about the safety of his uncle. But at this moment the schoolmaster seemed to have arrived at some sudden decision, for he struck his hand on the table.

" I'll do it," he said—" I'll do it ! Justice demands it. It's not right, it's not morally right that your uncle should be punished for a harmless kind of thing, and this man be let off. I see my way now. To-morrow is Saturday. I'll give the bairns the whole holiday, instead of

a half one, and I will go into Inverness and go
straight to his lordship's agent, Mr. MacInnes;
and if there's any one that ought to know that
there's smuggling going on on the Etherick
estate, Mr. MacInnes is the man.   It will cost
me something, Andrew, my lad; but *fiat justitia,
ruat cœlum.*   Let them say who like that there
is a spice of revenge in my trip, I care not.   To
catch a wheen trout was a small matter—it was
a mere idle amusement; but to be checked for
fishing without leave by this fellow—by this
fellow who is driving an illicit trade almost
within sight of the mansion-house, that is too
much!   We'll see what Mr. MacInnes will say
to that!"

The shock-headed schoolmaster seemed to
contemplate this projected journey of his with
great satisfaction, and of course Andrew Ross
eagerly welcomed anything that seemed likely
to be of aid to Donnacha Rua.   He did not
quite understand what the schoolmaster pro-
posed to do; but it was something, and surely
his interference would be for good.

"There's one thing I maun tell ye, Andrew,"
said the schoolmaster, after a few minutes'
consideration.   "It is your story that I am

taking in to Inverness. Now, I know every word of it is true, for I know you; but the people in Inverness, now, supposing they were to say, ' Oh, that is a fine story! It is natural that the lad Ross should bring such a charge against Big Murdoch, in order to get his uncle off; but how are we to know that it is true? If Big Murdoch says there is not a word of truth in it, what then?'"

Andrew Ross's face flushed. There was a kind of shame attached to the possibility of his being called upon to prove that he was not a liar.

"All that I can say," said he, "was that I heard Big Murdoch speaking as clearly as I hear you, and I heard Sandy and Pete, the gillies; and if people will not believe me, I cannot help it."

"But you could not make out their faces, Andrew?"

"I could not make out their faces because it was so dark," said the lad, rather sullenly.

"Well, now, Andrew, you need not look vexed with me," said his friend, "for I know that every word of your story is true. It is what the Inverness people will ask me that I am thinking of. And supposing, now, that they ask me whether you could take them to the black bothy, and show it to them, what am I to say to that?"

"Well," said the lad, "if they think that I should be able to take them straight to the bothy, perhaps I could not do that; for every one knows that such places are covered over and hidden; but this I am sure of—that, with a little time, I can find it out."

"It was all I wanted to ask you," said the schoolmaster, good-naturedly. "And now the bairns will be coming, I maun go over to the school-house. Do not be afraid, Andrew, I'll do what I can for your uncle. And I'm thinking your friend, Big Murdoch, will be dancing to another tune before many days are over."

And so the lad went away greatly comforted, if still anxious and only sorry that he could not convey to his uncle—away up there in the wilds of Allt-nam-ba—some idea of the intervention that was being made in his favour.

Early the next morning the schoolmaster set out from Edenbridge on his friendly mission; and what with a lift he obtained from a mail-cart for part of the way, and what with diligent walking, he managed to reach Inverness a little before noon. He went straight to the office of Mr. MacInnes, in the High Street, and was lucky enough to find that gentleman within. He was admitted to his private room, his name being known, and he was about to open his business, and make intercession on behalf of Donnacha Rua, when the lawyer—who did not look like a lawyer, by the way, for he was an immense, tall, white-headed, and broad-shouldered Highlander—interposed, and that in a sufficiently angry manner.

"God bless my soul, do not I know?" he exclaimed, and he smacked the back of his hand on to a sheet of paper that was lying before him on the table. "There—there it is. I got it this morning, and he would have me take out a summons against this shepherd. Now, Mr. Angus, you may not know—it is not your duty to know; but this I will tell you—that a keeper that quarrels with the shepherds is a fool, and does not know his business. I say he is a fool of a keeper, and not fit for his place. What is a roe-deer? Nothing. The useless animal would be away again before the winter, and there is none of the gentry there. It is not I that will complain of a shepherd taking a roe-deer, especially as you say it was not to sell it, but for the Widow Ross, that her ladyship was writing to me about no longer ago than yesterday. But what I complain of, Mr. Angus, is a keeper that is foolish enough to quarrel with the shepherds, when he should know that everything on a shooting depends on the good-will of the shepherds. Who can leave the nests alone in the spring? Who can keep in their dogs from chasing the young birds and the leverets? Who can give them notice when a stag is coming into the woods, instead of frightening him out again? I say to you, Mr. Angus, that a man who is not great friends with the shepherds is a fool, and not fit to be in the place a moment longer!"

The angry vehemence of the tall Highlander seemed entirely bent on the head of the poor schoolmaster; but he, seeing how well it served his turn, did not care to protest.

"Then you'll not be for taking out the summons, Mr. MacInnes?" he ventured to ask.

"I will *not* take out a summons!" he said, stamping his foot. "If I thought that Red Duncan, or any other one of them, was in the habit of poaching and selling the game, I would soon mend matters; I would have Colonel Graham dismiss him there and then; but you tell me yourself, Mr. Angus, that it was to give the poor widow woman a better mouthful—ay, and she just out of a fever—and what do you think his lordship would say to me if I was to make him a prosecutor in such a case, and have all the shepherds saying we were tyrants and cruel men, when they heard the story? Would that help us? Would that be better for the young grouse? Would that keep the woods any quieter?"

"Indeed, Mr. MacInnes," said the schoolmaster, "it was to ask you not to summons Donnacha Rua that I have come all the way in from Edenbridge; for he was only doing a kindly turn to his sister-in-law, that is very badly off; and I am sure he is no poacher; for I can answer for what the young lad Ross, that is a friend of mine, says of him; an' the young lad Ross and his mother are in poor circumstances since Big Murdoch brought the strange gillies to the place——"

"It was only yesterday," said Mr. MacInnes, looking among his papers, "that I had a letter from her ladyship directing me to say nothing about rent this year to the Widow Ross; and likewise that as there was no one at the lodge I was to provide that a bit present of game should be sent her from time to time; and I was waiting to see Murdoch myself, for he's an ill-conditioned, thrawn-necked, contentious, cantankerous kind of creature——"

"I can tell you something more about Big Murdoch, Mr. MacInnes," said the schoolmaster, who was not ill-pleased to learn in what estimation the keeper was held by the all-powerful agent. "Would ye be surprised to learn that Big Murdoch keeps a whisky-still going within a mile of Etherick Lodge?"

The tall Highlander stared—in a kind of dumbfounded way; and he stared in still greater amazement when the schoolmaster was giving him the full particulars of Andrew Ross's adventure. Indeed, he was far too astounded to give vent to either indignation or anger.

"The audahcity—the audahcity!" he kept repeating. "My certes, what will his lordship say to this?"

And then he turned sharp on the school master.

"How do ye know this story is true? Man, it's no possible! He wouldna dare. On the very edge of Etherick forest?—within sight o' the lodge?—The lad has invented the story to do Murdoch an ill turn for threatening his uncle."

"I expected that might be said," answered the schoolmaster, quietly, "though well I know that the lad is speaking the truth. However, it is an easy thing to show whether or no. He says he can find out the black bothy if he is allowed to search for it."

"And prove that Big Murdoch has had a hand in it," said the other suspiciously.

"Well, no; for that is asking too much, Mr. MacInnes. But I would have ye reflect on the matter. Do ye think it possible that any black bothy could be there—just on the outskirts of the forest—and him not know? A fine keeper that would be—to have such things happening under his nose! A fine watch he must have been keeping on the deer, when men could be coming and going, and sacks of malt, and barrels, and all the rest of it! And think of this, Mr. MacInnes—these things must have been coming and going by way of the loch——"

" In our own boat—in his lordship's own
boat ? " exclaimed Mr. MacInnes, in tones of
horror. " I never heard the like ! "

" Surely ye maun see it's no possible that
such things could be going on and Murdoch and
the rest of them be in ignorance of it ! Now, I
have been thinking of it, Mr. MacInnes, and this
is what I take to be fair—that if the lad can
take you, or me, or the supervisor, or any of the
officers, and find out the bothy, we are bound to
believe the rest. It's no likely ye'll find Big
Murdoch there—I should think not—a keeper's
eyes will soon tell him there are strangers on
the hills, or else he's no much of a keeper."

" I agree with ye, Mr. Angus ; I agree with
ye," the big Highlander said, with decision.
" If there is a still so near the forest as that,
it maun ha' been there wi' the knowledge o'
Murdoch and the gillies as well ; and the fair
presumption is that they are concerned in it. .
Eh, me, winna his lordship be an angry man at
such audahcity ! I never heard the like ! And
a fine change we made when we sent away John
Malcolm, that is a douce, honest, hard-working
fellow, to Glenelg, and put in his place this
thrawn-necked scoondrel. No, I will no say

that. I take back the word, Mr. Angus. Proof first is a lawyer's motto. But if this is true his lordship'll be making this country side too het for our neighbour Murdoch ; and I maun see that I am not remiss about acting on your information. Will ye oblige me, Mr. Angus, by stepping along with me to the Inland Revenue Office ? "

The schoolmaster was in nowise loth, for he had absolute confidence in the story that had been told him by Andrew Ross. But as they were walking along the street he ventured to say :

" Then, Mr. MacInnes, you will not be taking out the summons against the shepherd ? "

The answer was brief. It consisted in applying a phrase to the summons which was distinctly emphatic, but which was highly improper, and needs not therefore be repeated here.

CHAPTER V.

"THE HUNT IS UP."

IT was late that night when the schoolmaster got back to Edenbridge; but there was Andrew Ross anxiously waiting to hear the news.

"Well, Andrew," said he cheerfully, "ye may fling your bonnet in the air.   There is to be no summons."

"Is it you, then, that we have to thank for that?" said the lad.

"Me? Not one bit! Mr. MacInnes is a sensible man—he is for keeping on good terms with the shepherds.   He would not have taken out the summons in any case.   But that is only one-half of the business.   I had my own score to settle with Big Murdoch; and I'm thinking he'll have to pay—I'm thinking he'll have to pay."

The schoolmaster grinned and rubbed his hands; it was very clear that he had not forgotten his being prohibited from fishing in the Etherick burn.

"I shouldna wonder now, Andrew, lad," said he, more seriously, "if this turned out well for you. I had a talk with Mr. MacInnes, and he asked about you, and I assume that Lady Etherick was writing to him about your mother, and I told him how you were placed this year, and that it was a bad year for you, and you were thinking of going away to Glasgow. Now, tell me this, Andrew ; if you were to get work here, would you rather have that, or would you rather go away to Glasgow ?"

"I would rather be here," said the lad at once ; "for my mother is ill, and she does not like the thought of my going away. But if there was a certainty of work here, would it not be better than the chance of work in a great town ? But there is no hope of it that I can see."

"Do not be so sure," said the schoolmaster, mysteriously. "Mr. MacInnes was speaking to me about what his lordship would think of all this business, and that he might consider that you have done him a service—who knows? It is a fine thing to be in a position like his. You

nod your head, or say half a dozen words to
your agent, and you give someone a good place
and a good weekly wage at a moment's notice.
If his lordship thinks you have done him a
service, it's but a nod of the head and the thing
is done. But we'll not count on the chickens
before they are hatched, Andrew, my man. We
havena found the still yet."

"I do not know about the still," said young
Ross; "but this I know—that I can find the
black bothy."

"If you can make your way back to the
corrie you told me of," said the schoolmaster,
"that will be quite enough. There will be
others with you more accustomed to search for
such things than you. The supervisor will be
here the first thing on Monday morning, and
two or three of the officers with him, and maybe
Mr. MacInnes too; and if you can take them to
the corrie they will soon find out the rest—that
is, unless Big Murdoch has got some inkling and
has cleared out in the meantime. And now
good-night—for you must be getting home. Be
ready early on Monday morning. I do not
know what hour they may call at your mother's
cottage for you.

The lad still lingered, however.

"Mr. Angus," said he, with some hesitation, "I have been thinking I will go up to-morrow to Allt-nam-ba, to let my uncle know there is to be no summons. And if I was to wait until night and come round by the corrie again——"

"Why, you're daft, Andrew!" the other exclaimed, good-naturedly. "You would be running against some one or other of them, and then they would only give you a beating, and pack up their things and clear out, and there would be nothing to bring against them. No, no; keep as far away from the place as ye can until the officers go up with ye on Monday; then the sharper the work the better—though it's not to be expected ye'll find any o' them there. I was for advising a midnight raid, so as to catch them maybe; but the officers are against it in this case, it seems. They will be satisfied if they can destroy the apparatus, and they will find out the different places better in the daylight. As for Mr. MacInnes, if he finds a black bothy just on the outskirts of Etherick forest, there's no need to tell him who must have been working it, that's sure enough; and ye may depend on't that Big Murdoch and his gillies have taken their last look at this country side."

It was well done on the part of the school-master to conceal from Andrew Ross the fact that Mr. MacInnes had at first regarded his story with considerable suspicion, for that would only have made him nervous, whereas, when the party of officers called at the cottage in the gray dawn of the Monday morning, and he set out to guide them, he was quite confident that he could at least find the corrie, whatever they might discover afterwards. And as they proceeded to ascend the steep hillside, through a straggling wood of birch and rowan, Mr. MacInnes, who was also with them, began to question the lad more particularly as to how he had managed to stumble against Big Murdoch and his com-panions. Young Ross told the whole story frankly, confessing his share in that projected purloining of the deer, and though the tall High-lander, as was his duty, rebuked him smartly, still, there was no great severity in his tone.

"Your uncle should have known better than to lead a young lad like you into such a thing. But we will not say much about it, for it was not to sell the beast I am told——"

" Indeed it was not, sir," said the lad. " It was because he saw that my mother was not well since she had the fever."

" Well, well, we will not say any more about it ; but it is better for a young lad to keep out of such things, for who knows but that at any moment a situation might be offered him ? and there should be no stories of that kind attached to him. And maybe everything has happened for the best if we manage to dig out this wasps' byke of smugglers. That will be a good day's work whatever."

The Inland Revenue officers made no effort to conceal their approach. They were talking and laughing among themselves freely enough, though they were now clear of the woods and on the open heathery slopes forming the outskirts of the forest.* Probably they had no expectation of effecting a surprise, for they knew the nature of the country, and concluded that, if there were people at work in the black bothy, they would be sure to have some outlying scout ready to apprise them of any approaching danger. But what they next saw as they were going on in this free and easy fashion did astound

* There are no trees in a Highland deer forest.

them in no small measure. Quite suddenly a
man stood before them. He seemed to have
jumped out of the earth, so unexpected was his
appearance ; and even Mr. MacInnes, who recognised the stranger to be one of the gillies, for
a second or two regarded him as if he were an
apparition.

" What are you doing here ? " said MacInnes
rather angrily.

The small, broad-shouldered, Celtic-looking
man answered with some sulkiness :

" I was setting a trap, sir."

" Let me see it," said the agent, who had his
suspicions.

But there, true enough, was the trap, very
artfully laid, and the gillie added, as if to con-
firm his story :

" I saw a dog-fox come by here on Saturday
morning."

" Is Big Murdoch at the lodge ? " said Mac-
Innes, looking at the man sharply.

The gillie betrayed no concern, he only glanced
from one to the other of the officers, as he said :

" Oh yes, sir. I think he will be at the lodge."

" Then go down and tell him not to go away
anywhere until I see him."

"Very well, sir," said the man, setting off with much self-possession, as one of the officers said to the other :

"That fellow was there to give some signal, as sure as you're alive."

It was almost directly after this that they struck the head of the small ravine they were in search of. At least Andrew Ross made sure that this was the corrie ; and having descended it for some little distance he came in sight of the loch, just as he had expected. And now a general search began. He gave them a guess as to the whereabouts of the bothy ; but, naturally, it was only a guess. They began to pry behind boulders and push aside bushes, even to sound the heather. Andrew Ross was as active as any of them ; but in the end, as it proved, the discovery was not to be his. All at once one of the officers uttered a short, low whistle, and then they could see him push aside some branches of a small birch tree, and then step over one or two large pieces of rock.

"I don't know whether the wasps are inside, Mr. MacInnes," said he facetiously ; "but here's the byke."

Of course there was a general rush to the

Q

place, and the officer who had made the discovery, after taking a box of matches from his
pocket, lifted aside a rude kind of door that had
been constructed of two or three planks nailed
together, with a most ingenious coating of
heather, grass, and ferns glued on to it, and
passed on by the dark aperture that was thus
disclosed. The others lost no time in following
him, and presently there was a glow of light in
the cavern which they got into, for the first
visitor had now lit a candle. This recess they
were now exploring had probably been in the
first place of natural formation, and not more
than four or five feet deep ; but the ingenuity of
the smugglers, having perceived the opportune-
ness of this entrance, had easily succeeded in
clearing out behind a large space admirably
adapted for their illicit trade. And here was all
the apparatus necessary for that trade, though
there was no trace of recent occupation, and not
a single jar or barrel of whisky there. The still
seemed a comparatively new one, and so also the
copper worm ; these the officers said they would
have to take to the Inland Revenue Office at
Inverness. But the fermenting casks which
they found standing they instantly proceeded to

demolish ; and the task took no great time. All this while Mr. MacInnes stood looking on like one amazed.

" The audahcity of it—the audahcity of it ! " he kept exclaiming. "Almost within sight of the lodge ! Did ever any one hear the like ? "

The detective officers, however, had not nearly done. In the course of another hour or so, their close and diligent searching of this corrie, from the very top of it down almost to the loch, had disclosed to them no fewer than three other places of concealment, each furnished with its own supply of stores—ropes and pulleys, casks, sacks of malt, and what not, all of which were instantly confiscated. And then, when they had satisfied themselves that they had thoroughly dug out that wasps' byke, they playfully suggested to Mr. MacInnes that he and they together could do no better than proceed to Etherick Lodge to see whether Big Murdoch could not afford them some entertainment in the way of breakfast. Mr. MacInnes was for going on to Etherick Lodge, but in no such humorous mood. There could be no manner of doubt that this black bothy had belonged to Big Murdoch

Q 2

and his allies. It was impossible for this thing to have been going on without his knowing well of it, and he certainly would not have risked his situation to allow other people to carry on an illicit still on the very edge of Lord Etherick's house. The audacity of it—this was what overwhelmed the mind of Mr. MacInnes; and while he consented to go on to the lodge, it was with no facetious hopes of breakfast. He was in doubt as to which would be the more appropriate mood for the forthcoming interview—indignant, anger or sardonic sarcasm. One thing he was determined on at least—that Big Murdoch and his gillies should have instant and peremptory dismissal, bag and baggage.

Of that interview, however, which proved to be a somewhat stormy one, Andrew Ross was not a spectator. His part in the business was over.

"Ye may go back home now, my lad," Mr. MacInnes said to him; "and I think I may tell ye that his lordship will be obliged to ye for this service. I hear ye were sometimes at the lodge when John Malcolm was there."

"Oh yes, sir, every autumn, and sometimes in the winter too."

"And they tell me ye have learned something about the breaking in of dogs."

"I hope, sir, I know a little of that, for it is little I know of anything else," was the modest reply.

"Well, ye must not be thinking that his lordship has to turn every young lad about here into a keeper to prevent his being a poacher; but when I get John Malcolm up from Glenelg, I will see what he says about ye. And you can tell your mother that her ladyship was writing about her, and she need not think any more about the rent for this year; and maybe if I find that the roe-deer that was near getting Donnacha Rua into trouble is to the fore yet, there may be a bit of it find its way to the cottage."

And so young Ross set out home with a light heart, and gave the messages to his mother; but he said nothing about the mysterious hints with regard to himself that had fallen from Mr. MacInnes, for he knew not what they might mean.

It was about a week after that that he definitely learned. He was at work in the little patch of potato garden adjoining the cottage, when a dog-cart came driving along, and stopped. Then there was a sharp whistle, and instantly he put down his spade and went to the roadside. It was Lord Etherick himself—a little, thin, wiry, gray-haired man—who was in the dog-cart; so Andrew quickly touched his cap, as in duty bound.

" You are Andrew Ross—eh ? " said his lordship, who spoke rapidly and sharply, and had a habit of answering his own questions. " Much obliged to you, my lad, for putting us on the scent of those impudent scoundrels. Has John Malcolm gone by this morning ? No ? "

" No, your lordship."

" You'll see him in the afternoon most likely, then. He is a friend of yours, I take it ? Well, you've done him a good turn by getting rid of Murdoch. Malcolm will be head keeper now, and he will see that your mother hasn't to set the shepherds poaching. How is the poor woman ? Much the same, I suppose ? Here, take this parcel ; it's from her ladyship."

He handed out of the dog-cart a large tin box, which young Ross took in his arms.

" You're good friends with Malcolm—eh ? Yes ; I guessed that. He spoke well of you.

He says you're smart with the dogs. You may be under-keeper, if you like, at the lodge, take charge of the kennels, and have a pound a week. Would you like it? Is that enough? Eh— what?"

" It is a very good wage, indeed, your lordship," said young Ross, who was rather breathless.

" Speak to Malcolm about it," his lordship continued, in the same rapid way. " Is that your sister, the little girl with the cow? Yes; I thought so. Tell her not to keep the cow by the roadside. Drive her down to the meadows by the bridge, and get her fattened up a bit. Say I said so ; do you understand?"

And therewith he drove on again, leaving young Ross rather amazed and stupefied by his sudden good fortune. But the horse had not gone a dozen yards when he was pulled up, and his lordship called back

" Hi, look here, my lad! No more of that snaring of roe-deer, do you understand? You are a keeper now, remember."

" Yes, your lordship," said Andrew Ross, dutifully, though it may be doubted if he knew at that precise moment whether he was standing on his head or his heels.

And then it suddenly occurred to him that it was high time that this wonderful news should be carried into the cottage. No such welcome tidings had been taken thither for many and many a day.

THE END.

LONDON: PRINTED BY WM. CLOWES AND SONS, LIMITED,
STAMFORD STREET AND CHARING CROSS.

www.ingramcontent.com/pod-product-compliance
Lightning Source LLC
Chambersburg PA
CBHW020117030726
47498CB00006B/2144